After These Things

JENNY DISKI

A *Virago* Book

First published in Great Britain in 2004 by Little, Brown
This edition published in 2005 by Virago Press

Copyright © Jenny Diski 2004

The moral right of the author has been asserted

A CIP catalogue record for this book
is available from the British Library

ISBN 1 84408 015 3

Typeset in Horley by M Rules
Printed and bound in Great Britain by Clays Ltd, St Ives plc

Virago Press
An imprint of
Time Warner Book Group UK
Brettenham House
Lancaster Place
London WC2E 7EN

www.virago.co.uk

F125, 169
€10.00

Jenny Diski was born in 1947 in London, where she lived and worked for most of her life. She is the author of eight novels, including *Only Human* and *Nothing Natural* which are published by Virago; a collection of short stories and two books of essays as well as two bestselling memoirs, *Stranger on a Train*, winner of the J. R. Ackerley Award for Autobiography for 2003 and The Thomas Cook Travel Book Award 2003 and *Skating to Antarctica*, both published by Virago. She now lives in Cambridge.

Also by Jenny Diski

NOVELS

Rainforest
Like Mother
Happily Ever After
Monkey's Uncle
Then Again
The Dream Mistress
Only Human
Nothing Natural

SHORT STORIES

The Vanishing Princess

MEMOIR

Skating to Antarctica
Stranger on a Train

ESSAYS

Don't
A View from the Bed and Other Observations

I the Lord thy God am a jealous God, visiting the iniquity of the fathers upon the children . . .

Exodus 20:5

The fathers shall not be put to death for the children, neither shall the children be put to death for the fathers: every man shall be put to death for his own sin.

Deuteronomy 24:16

So finally, after several botched attempts, humankind beat the Lord at the story game and the Lord sulked mightily, as would any creation, thought up and disturbed into existence and then disputed with by the very creatures whom He thought He had invented. A great long lordly sulk there was after Abraham bound his boy, challenging and defeating God-the-Narrator with the threat of the premature end of His own story. God clammed up. Certainly there were times later when the children of Abraham liked to think that the Lord spoke directly to them too, as children would, but He did not walk and eat and dicker with them for the lives of the Sodomites, as He had with Abraham; He only ever came in dreams to them. And what are dreams if not the stories humans tell themselves, their wishes made phantom-real? Night-children born out of the desire to be heard, to make sense, to get the attention they believe they deserve. If the father deserved it, why not the son? God, it was said, spoke directly only one more time, generations after the

1

children of Abraham, to another chosen individual in His sadly self-revealing attempt to make Himself palpable to His creation, or creators, what you will.

And more like an affliction than a triumph, humanity's stories, the narration humans had wrenched from the deity, came and came. Counterpointing, contradicting, refining, refuting, relating, distorting, destroying, deceiving, denying, explaining, excusing, blaming, boasting. Depending on who was doing the telling and who the listening. As if anyone ever stops telling for long enough to listen. And, we might wonder, is the telling really intended for another to listen to, so often is it done in silence and alone? Who could have made such consciousnesses up? Creatures like all the others that creep and crawl and pad and thunder over the earth, with all their needs and functions, but who uniquely weld together bits of stuff – memory, fantasy and dream – into *stories*. *Homo fabulans*. What is the wordless, blank-minded baby doing all those crying, sucking, excreting months but waiting for language and building its story reservoir?

So when folks made up the cracking tale of creation and its creator, they proceeded to vie with that creator for control of story, and won, of course, for how could they lose? It's what they do, the only thing they can do with all the time and all the knowing they're stuck with. The past, present and future squat in their heads waiting to be filled in with narrative.

And once the story became theirs, the humans told it over and over, to themselves mostly, as I say, trying to get it straight, or just idling the time away. Version after version; story without end. In the beginning, they began. And so it came to pass, they continued. And in the end, they ended. And then began again. Repeating or altering, it didn't matter, so long as the narrative

2

trickled on inside their heads, and spilled out of their mouths, and fell upon their ears. The great chaos of telling it as it is, or might be or could never be, but telling, telling, telling. *Tell me a story. A true story. Make a story up. This happened, really happened to me. And then, and then and then. And so that is why. And that is how it came about. And this is my story. And mine. And mine. And have you forgotten his story? And her story? And. And. And . . .*

And nothing, finally. Because after the last gasp, all the stories are lost. The light goes out, the story ends, usually in mid-sentence.

And if someone were to listen in to the stories each of them told of themselves and their relation to others, and were to present them together, a compilation, what might emerge? Another version. Let's go no further than that. Just another story to add to the mountainous heap. Let's not talk about truth, or any other such foolishness. And what would this god-like character be, listening in, cutting and pasting, re-shaping, juxtaposing, adding a little here, taking something away there? With no story of his or her own to tell? Hardly. Such a one has never been. Let's say an editor – a redactor. Someone with a story to tell about stories.

And then again, people get stuck. They want stories but they find themselves in the thrall of a single moment, a point around which they revolve, spun helplessly by an attraction to some, as they perceive it, central event which has, you might say, bewitched them. A pivotal moment. One that takes you by the throat and won't be thought through, only round and round. No resolution comes, no movement forward. The story seems to vanish along with the time the narrative creates. There is just the identification with the moment, or period, before which everything was different, or after which nothing was the same. The *moment* enchants the teller precisely because it has implications for the rest of the story, yet it retards the narrative, cripples it. The moment is everything. A brief vision stands for everything and nothing. The story stutters to a stop without ever coming to a conclusion. Stuck. So these compulsive storytellers lose their story to an overwhelming moment, as if the material itself takes over from the narrator and demands deference. Or is it merely a lack of courage on the part of the tellers? The fear that the story will turn out nothing more than ordinary, anodyne. Better stay with the dramatic moment than confront the overall blandness of one's single go at existence, the disappointment of retrospection, the ineluctability of the conclusion, which, in any case, the teller will not be present to tell of. A collusion, of course, between enthralment and paralysis, and an unwillingness to face the structure. And so editors become necessary.

Editors are as obsessed about structure as the individual storyteller is obsessed about his or her *moments*. Editors patch and refit the various stories, each stuck in their various moments, into an order of some kind, so as to come to a conclusion. Where would humanity be without conclusions? Revolving round and round their separate points, dancing some crazed unchoreographed dance, singing single notes, caterwauling an unorchestrated cacophony. Him fixated on his moment, her on hers, but never thinking that both their moments, and all the others, belong together to make an (if you like) accidental structure, something else, something astonishingly different from all the individual moments.

So us editors? We just put things together and see if they

4

make . . . anything. We take the solitary *I*, and replace it with the third person. Of course, you have to interfere a little. It's true that juxtaposing one version with another has a certain quiet effect, creating a reading between the lines which is the result of the editor's manipulation, but there is more to do than that. In any case what story is not the editor's story? And this story is certainly mine. Mine as much as anyone's.

1

Death for him was never more than a heart's beat away. Every breath the final one. Every meal his last. Nothing, therefore, was more worthy of his attention than the strength of the pounding in his chest, the depth of his latest inhalation and the tastiness of food in his mouth. Only these things assured him he was alive, for now, at least. He had known for many years, decades, almost a lifetime how close death was. Closer than breath, closer than love, closer than future. It was the lesson he learned as a lad, and having learned it, it filled his existence. And once he had discovered so convincingly that death was just an instant away, he was unable to learn anything else.

Yet as close as death was to him all his days, he had nonetheless reached an age when the world should have regarded him as an elder worthy of respect. A husband, a father, the head of a family and a household of substantial wealth. But all of this, he knew, as he knew about death, was from his father, or because of him. Of Abraham.

Now Isaac was blind and bedridden, at an age when his father had not yet engendered him, let alone six out of his seven half-brothers. Only the first half-brother had been born to Abraham before he reached the age Isaac was now. *Ishmael*, Abraham's firstborn. The only one that mattered.

Isaac reclined on a low bed, bundled in layers of robes and woollen shawls, and covered with rugs against the cool, early morning air, but he trembled, it seemed to him with cold, fingering and feebly tugging at the cloth round his shoulders as if no amount of covering could keep him warm.

'Rebekah . . . Rebekah . . .' His voice was high-pitched and querulous. 'Rebekah . . .'

But Rebekah was already there, standing beside him, looking down at the elderly man. She said nothing. Isaac raised his head and seemed to sniff the air.

'Are you there? Where are you, woman?'

He peered hard in the direction of the open tent flap, where she stood in the light of the dawn rising behind her. She was nothing more to his failed sight than a patch of denser fog amid the darkness.

'Yes, yes, what is it?' she said finally.

'Were you here?'

'I am now.'

'Fetch the boy. It's important. Bring him to me now.'

'Which boy?'

'I'm a sick man.' Rebekah looked unimpressed. 'I must see him. Bring Esau to me.'

'Ah, that boy.'

'I'm sick. I haven't got much time left.'

'So you've been saying since we were first married.'

'But now I'm old.'

8

Rebekah conceded that with a raised eyebrow and pursed lips.

'There are plenty older. What do you want with Esau?'

'Just send him to me. It's my business.'

'Men's business?'

'Death's business.'

'Why not Jacob? He's in my tent having breakfast.'

'Bring Esau. Bring him now. Now.' The voice rose to a petulant squawk.

Rebekah shrugged and left.

Isaac sank back on to his pillows. He groaned and pulled the edges of his shawls tighter around himself. His heartbeat was a mere flutter, the breaths he took would not have kept a bird alive, and in his mouth there was only the faint taste of bitterness.

Outside, Rebekah roused the servant who sat on a low bench set against the wall of the tent, and sent him to find Esau. She remained where she was, just outside the opening to the tent, and with an exasperated sigh sank heavily onto the vacated bench. She wondered if Isaac was indeed dying. She didn't think so. He had been dying so often, for so long. He was fading, that was true; his eyesight was gone, he was too weak, or too will-less, to leave his bed. But he had been fading for as long as she had known him. She thought he would not die exactly when his time came, but gutter and go out like a lamp whose light was already so feeble that the darkness would hardly be increased when it finally failed. Sometimes, looking at him, she felt he was becoming invisible, for all his grumbling and demands. Visibility had never been his strong point, except for that first moment, when she saw him from a distance,

9

walking slowly, head down, alone in a field, going nowhere, and she discovered that he was her destination. It might have been a dream, but it turned out to be the beginning of the life she had been waiting to lead. Not that it was the life she thought she had been waiting for, but it was the one she got. You only get one, and so young. Such a very long time to have to lead it. Panic, her close companion, rose in her, a black whirlwind that spiralled up from somewhere deep in her belly and swirled into her head so that she felt as if she were spinning aimlessly in a black empty sky or burrowing through numberless grains of sand. The old scream was forcing its way into her throat – *Why? Why me?* – the scream that had never received a satisfactory answer and which she now suppressed with a single furious groan.

Isaac waited in his personal darkness for his son to arrive. His present fear of death was so great that he would have run from it, blind and feeble as he was, but he knew that there was nowhere to go. No place of safety. No one to protect him. This was what he had learned. Once, in that first encounter with death, he might have run for it, but he didn't. He walked on, step by step towards death without protest. A stupefied boy. A stupid boy. Not to protest at going to his own execution. Obedient, paralysed, disbelieving, suicidal; whatever his state, it was unforgivable, he now saw, to volunteer himself for death. And death had been with him ever since. His whole life since that first dying had been lived in fear of the next and final dying. His eyesight, his bodily strength, his mind had all been dimmed his whole life by the blazing light of the revelation of his own death.

*

He knew, even from the moment when his father woke him and told him to get ready for the hunting trip he had suggested the night before, that something wasn't right. Abraham looked like death himself; he spoke only three single syllables.

'We must go.'

A hunting trip, son and father, was a holiday. It merited a smile. But Abraham's mouth was a rigid line within his steely grey surrounding beard. His furrowed brow-shaded eyes refused to meet those of his waking son. As soon as Isaac's eyelids opened, his father left the tent and made busy with the donkey, saddling it himself rather than let the two lads who were to accompany them do it. They stood around looking useless, and also puzzled as they saw the same inappropriate look on Abraham's face that Isaac glimpsed. They shrugged at one another. An argument with the mistress perhaps. That satisfied them. Isaac up and watching his father, too, knew, though he didn't know why he knew, it wasn't any dispute with Sarah that caused his father's odd expression. When the donkey was ready, Abraham took an axe and began splitting logs. His arm rose and hovered above his head for a moment before it fell weightily and the axe sliced through the log, causing its two halves to leap away to either side. Isaac watched the deliberation of his father's movements. There was none of the light repeated rhythm that usually accompanied the swinging of the axe. Each blow was separate and considered. The pause at the top of his swing getting longer each time. And it was clear to Isaac that this was not to be the uncomplicated hunting trip his mother had approved the evening before.

They left without a word spoken. Just a nod from Abraham that it was time to go. Isaac supposed his mother was still asleep, it was well before dawn. They went on in silence. Abraham on

11

the donkey, Isaac on foot beside him, the pale obedient son, and the servants walking behind, but not talking to each other, as they would do normally. Abraham's stiff, straight back kept them silent. It was known, of course, that Abraham received personal instructions from his Lord, the only Lord the family and its retinue was now permitted to worship. This Lord whispered his wishes and promises into Abraham's ear alone. But his present silence was not that of a man who was listening, but of someone intent on completing a task without permitting the slightest distraction from the world.

And not a word was spoken. Not one word all that day. They stopped to eat and made camp for the night merely on more nods of Abraham's head. His silence was so intense that no one dared impose a sound on it. Isaac's docile muteness was to be expected, but even the servant boys, whose discomfort without talk was extreme, only dared make perplexed and discontented faces at each other. In the morning Abraham shook the three lads awake and they set off again on their journey without a word.

And another day passed in silence.

On the third day, towards noon, Abraham pulled his donkey up, in the shadow of Mount Moriah. But instead of getting down to indicate it was time for lunch, he remained where he was for a long while, staring up at the mountain. Isaac looked into his father's face and saw his gaze, steady, unblinking, as drained of emotion as he had ever seen any countenance. His spirit shrivelled with fear.

Abraham stepped down from the donkey and led it back towards the boys. He did not look at Isaac as he passed. At last, he broke his silence.

'You lads stay with the donkey. The boy and I will walk up

into the mountain to make a sacrifice to the Lord. Wait for us here.'

Still saying nothing to his son, Abraham took the wood he had split and put it in Isaac's cradling arms. He himself took the burning torch to light the wood, and a cleaver, and father and son went on together, wordlessly, up into the mountain.

Rebekah had not returned to her tent; she remained sitting on the servant's bench staring down at her dusty sandalled feet. She was just resting, she told herself, taking the load off her legs to relieve the pain that ran from deep inside her buttock down through her left thigh if she put weight on it, and made her limp heavily much of the time. And her head hurt, as usual, with that pain like thumbs pressing down viciously on her brow above her eyes, and the immense strain at the back of her skull where her neck met her head, as if she were weighted down with a yoke. She came to consciousness with the pain most days, and fell asleep – eventually – with it most nights. No one knew what it was like, the monstrous hurts that pounded inside her head and radiated through her pelvis, and which she could never get away from. She had tried all manner of herbs and concoctions, but nothing could relieve her discomfort. She was elderly and people assumed that the elderly *had* discomforts, that they were invalids by virtue of their years to some degree or other. It was normal. But that was not how it felt to Rebekah. She was imprisoned in an alien body with its pains. She could not accept that this was her life; that the pain was hers; her daily lot. That she was not young any more, that so much of her life had already been lived was yet another aspect of her pain. She did not see why she should have to accept suffering – still. Yet there seemed no remedy available, only the end of life itself, and sometimes she thought that would be preferable to continuing the way it was. The way it had been for so long. Her life. She wanted to weep, weep or scream, when she thought those words. Her life. All there was. All there would be. Her single, only life, which now, in her final decades – if she lasted so long – would not change in any way. Nothing new would happen, nothing that would make the words 'my life' mean more than bitter disappointment and a shocking sense of unfairness.

She had felt no pain the day when life announced that it was about to begin. The day the waiting was over and her true life was going to start. No pain, no great lumbering body, no heavy lines pulling the sides of her mouth down to her slacking jaw. Another person. When she remembered herself back then, it was perfectly possible to reinhabit the blooming, energetic, fresh girl's body she once had. She felt that body and the person in it to be more real than anything she had been since. How astonishing that such change can happen to a person, day by day, creeping, spreading so that there was never any one moment when she could look at herself in a reflecting surface and say: this is a new me. She always seemed to be herself, each day the same as the last; and yet how she was now, and how she was then . . . As if there were two distinct people. But that was not so, because she still *felt* the sensations of the girl who, without thinking of the effort involved, had carried her water jug lightly to the well, pleased to be walking in the gathering dusk, accepting the slight cooling breeze on her cheeks as her rightful pleasure, her legs pain-free, strong and always ready to break into a run, her head and shoulders light and ignorant of any pressure at all. She remembered being that, remembered the swing of her hips, the mixture of excitement and impatience on waking each day, the sense that anything could and would happen. Was it really like that? No dark spaces, no resentment, a body that did her will and willed activity for its own sake?

Not quite. She did not greatly care for her family, controlled, since her father's death, by her ever-calculating oldest brother and an acquiescent mother who looked to him for every decision. They were quite settled in their existence, their lives where and what they were. Middling people in the middle of a small town. So small. They wanted more, were always planning and plotting to increase their lot, but it was more of the same they wanted. Rebekah's life belonged elsewhere, in another place, with another family. It was the way of the world. A young girl grows up waiting for change. She waits to be taken to somewhere new, away from her land, her birthplace and her father's house, to be clothed in new status in the company of strangers who become her life and her future. For some that held terror, to be taken away from the familiar, or to have to come to terms with the fact that a lack of beauty and a dull personality might oblige her to accept a new family who could do no better than her. But Rebekah had no such fears, she knew her very youth and energy made her desirable. And in any case she *was* beautiful. She longed confidently for the invisible future that was the way of the world and which would come and collect her. She never doubted that her looks and her zest would win her a better family than the one she had been born into, and wanted nothing more than to turn her back on her rapacious, overbearing brother whose eyes were dim with his own limitations and only lit up when thoughts of wealth in order to acquire more of the same came into his head. So perhaps her life then was not perfect. She felt no affection for her family, no pleasure in their company. They were a group of individuals each focused on themselves. To them she was the daughter who had a chance of catching a husband who could pay a decent bride price. Well, they were welcome to it, providing her life was also improved. She despised them for their paltry ambitions. She longed to be somewhere that she perceived as the centre of things, with people who embraced life and its opportunities. Love would be no bad thing either, if it happened to come along. If she was not presently enclosed by a wall of love, she had hopes, and hopes were strong enough to make her step light and her lips curl into a smile.

Not that the old man sitting wearily with his back against one of his kneeling camels by the well looked much like a promise of future. It was nearing dusk and time for the daughters of the townsmen to collect and carry the water for the night and morning ahead back to their family. But she was the first to arrive. She ran down the steps, filled her jug from the spring and walked back up with the jug hoist on one shoulder. She was aware of the stranger watching her as she emerged. He was standing now, grey with the dust and grime of travelling, and began to come towards her.

'Please,' he called. 'A sip of water from your jug?'

His voice crackled with thirst, but he was too old and too tired to gather water for himself. Rebekah felt a surge of sympathy. It was pitiful to be so slow, so incapable of fulfilling your own needs. Her heart went out to him and she ran towards him to stop him having to make the extra effort to reach her. Somehow, her legs were all the stronger, the weight of the jug full of slopping water all the slighter for her awareness of the old man's frailty. She felt that he would be heartened by her energy and youth, as if just the sight of her had curative powers.

She smiled at him, beaming goodwill and pity for his old age, and lowered the jug onto her palm, holding it aslant so that he could collect water in his cupped hands and drink all he wanted. When he finished he wiped his mouth and looked directly into her face. She was surprised that he seemed to be waiting, as if her donation of water, her smile and simple kindness were not enough. He said nothing. She gestured with the jug to offer him more, but he shook his head, his eyes boring into her. What else did he want? What else did he think he had the right to expect? She was confused. Then one of the row of kneeling camels behind the man snorted. The old man turned his face very slightly at the sound. Rebekah looked at them for a moment, and then smiled happily again. There was more she could do, more life and vigour she could delight the old man with.

'You just sit and rest and I'll draw water for your camels.'

The weariness dropped from his face. He looked at her now as if she were a marvellous apparition, and then with an expression of relief, he nodded, closing his eyes, though it wasn't clear whether he was nodding his agreement with her plan to water the camels, or acknowledging something to someone who was invisible to Rebekah. His excessive pleasure in her offer spurred her on to a prodigious effort. He had ten camels with him, and after their long desert journey, from who knew where, they were parched. Gallons of water were needed for each one. Rebekah raced down the steps of the well, scooping water into her jug and emptying it again and again into the trough, hardly pausing before running back to get more. She almost flew, her energy demonic, almost superhuman. She delighted in the image she had of herself, blurred with speed, sprinting back and forth, feeling endless capacity at her disposal and basking in the

17

wonder and gratitude of the old man as the camels slurped at the trough. Nothing would stop her until every camel had turned its disdainful back and found a shady spot to settle down for a well-earned rest. It was not that she loved camels especially, but that she loved herself and all her promise and the life to come, and she knew that the great wide world would love her too. It gave her miraculous powers.

When she had at last finished, she bent over, her hands on her knees, panting to catch her breath. She looked up at the man and laughed at her effort and her exhaustion. He came towards her holding something in his hand.

'What family are you from? Does your father have room to put us up for the night?' he asked as he held out to her a heavy gold ring and two wide gold bracelets.

Rebekah stared at the jewellery overflowing in her cupped hands. In the gathering darkness they gleamed bright and soft, buttery gold, richer than anything she had ever held in her hands before. She remembered eventually that she had been asked a question.

'Bethuel. My father was Bethuel. He was the son of Milcah and Nahor. He is dead. My brother, Laban, is head of the family now. We have plenty of feed for your camels and room for you and your servants.'

And the old man gasped as she spoke the name of her father and grandparents. He covered his face with his hands and murmured, 'Thanks be to the Lord of Abraham, for leading me to my master's own family in my search.'

Rebekah could hardly hear what he said. She caught the name Abraham. Her grandfather had had a brother called Abraham, who long long ago had gone his own way and not been heard of since. But her mind was whirling with the shining

18

presents she held in her hands and the thrilling feel of life running at full speed straight towards her.

It was Isaac who broke the silence eventually after they had
been walking for hours and long since lost sight of the two lads
waiting with the donkey.

'Father?'

'Here I am, my son.'

'You're carrying the fire and the cleaver, and I've got the
wood. But I don't see any sheep for the sacrifice.'

'The Lord will see to the sheep for the sacrifice, my son.'

Isaac received no comfort from the sound of his father's
voice. He seemed not to be speaking to him, but growling to the
air around them, his words reverberating in the silence like
approaching thunder. He was threatening, but threatening who?
Not Isaac; it was as if Isaac no longer existed for Abraham. He
was threatening his Lord, Isaac understood. His whole being
was engaged with the Lord whom only he had access to. All his
silence, and his grim, set face since their journey started, had
been directed at his Lord, as if the two of them were doing
battle so fierce that no words could be expended. And the battle
ground? But Isaac knew.

They stopped, and Abraham set to work. Isaac had never
experienced such aloneness, a speck lost in a world that had no
use for him, that found him pointless and irrelevant except for
a single value – that he was his father's son, that he was the consequence of his father's Lord's promise. Who was there to cry
out to for help as he stood with his arms cradling the wood that
his father now took piece by piece and laid in criss-cross preci-
sion on the altar he had just built? Who was there in the world
to defend him when his father led him forward – as without

19

question or resistance he allowed his father to lead him – and laid him down on top of the wooden pyre? No cry of his would reach his mother. And there was no one else to hear him apart from his father and the Lord, who seemed intent on listening only to each other. He might have run away; Abraham was old, Isaac was young and faster. But there was no fraction of a second when such an idea occurred to him. To run away would have been to admit that his father intended to harm him. And until he lay voluntarily on the altar and could no longer avoid the truth, he refused the idea. Eventually, he spoke.

'Father,' looking up at the old man who held his head high and his eyes averted. 'Father, what will you tell mother?'

Not 'How can you do this to me, your son, your favourite son?' Not 'What kind of father are you to kill your child?' Not 'Don't touch me, you treacherous murderer, or I'll tear that knife out of your hand and sink it into your heart.' But 'What will you tell mother?' Assuming the deed already done. Assuming there was no escape, no chance of further life. No mercy even for a son as innocent as milk.

His father did not answer. Isaac looked up at the cloudless sky and tried to scream, because even a mountain was witness to the fact that his obedient father was going to kill him as he had been told to by a god whom no one but Abraham himself had seen or heard. But no sound came. Isaac's throat was locked. His mouth was filled with sand. He opened it in a shocked 'O', but nothing broke the silence. He tried to shut his eyes against the sight of his father looming over him, but his eyelids had lost their ability to blink. So Isaac stared up at the aching blue sky above him directly into the scorching sun and his eyes began to overflow, drenched with something more caustic than tears, something that burned and stung and then seared with a pain of sharpened sticks being twisted in his eyeballs. These acid tears clouded the blue of Isaac's pupils with a pale, milky scarring, like the cataracts of the old, blinding him, so that he sensed rather than saw his father reach for the cleaver on the ground and then knew, but did not see, that Abraham had raised his arm high above his head where it paused to take careful aim. And Isaac waited, blinded in his blackness, then and now, young and old, his flesh on fire and quivering with expectation, for the inevitable death blow to be dealt.

There was no need for Rebekah to stretch out her arms to show her family the presents she had received from the old man. Laban, her brother, would have known about them even if she had kept them firmly behind her back. He would have seen through her flesh and bone to the glint of gold. As he held her wrists to examine the bracelets she saw the quality of the gold reflected in the gleam in her brother's eyes. He walked dreamily past her towards the old man with his retinue of camels and servants.

'Please, please come in. Do us the honour of staying with us. Let me help you.'

Laban ushered them towards the house, ordered stabling for the camels, and water to bathe the feet of their keepers. He barked at servants to bring food. But the old man shook his head.

'Wait, let me speak. I am Eliezer, the servant of Abraham, who was the brother of Nahor, your grandfather. He has become very wealthy, and his son, Isaac, will inherit everything. He sent me to find a wife for Isaac among his own people. I thought, how can I choose a wife for my master's son, and so I left it up to the God of Abraham, deciding that I would wait by a well and see if a woman came and offered to water my camels. A test, you see. It would be a sign that she was the one. And Rebekah, your daughter, came and did exactly that. The God of Abraham led me directly to this girl from his brother's family. So will you agree to the betrothal of Rebekah and Isaac?'

Eliezer had barely time to draw breath before Laban nodded his enthusiastic agreement to the plan.

'Yes, yes, it's obviously destined. Your God of Abraham wants this marriage to be. Who are we to stand in such a god's way?'

He looked towards Rebekah's mother for her approval. She nodded her head in the same rhythm as her son. And although she might have wondered why her suitor had not come to find her himself, Rebekah's heart soared as she watched her family hand her over to the stranger. She was to be free at last. She was to begin her real existence.

That night there was great feasting and drinking. Eliezer presented the family with more gifts he had brought and a rich bride price was negotiated. During a quiet moment Rebekah asked Eliezer about her new family and husband-to-be.

'Isaac is the son of Abraham and Sarah's old age. He was promised by the Lord, Abraham's Lord. He is the first in what will become a great nation.'

'Does Abraham have only the one Lord?'

'One very jealous Lord, who blessed him and his house greatly for recognising him and worshipping him alone.'

'And Isaac's mother, Sarah?'

'Is dead. Abraham remarried and had children, but only the son of Sarah will receive his blessing and inheritance. He is the promised son. Abraham was ailing when I left. Isaac is the line, and you are to be his Sarah.'

'And Isaac . . .'

'A very quiet man. I mean, he doesn't say much. Hesitant, perhaps. He needs someone of his own, and with your energy, your vivacity, he would blossom, I'm sure. Yes, I'm certain he would.'

Rebekah had no doubt of it, just as she had had no doubt that life would scoop her up and take her to where she herself would blossom. And wasn't that exactly what was about to happen? She imagined her quiet husband just waiting to be touched by her beauty and youth. Too sweet, too shy to come himself and choose a bride. A quiet man was good. All manner of things might be going on inside a quiet man. A quiet man might be a very satisfactory husband. She would bring him out of himself. It's a sad thing when a man loses his mother, but she could make it up to him. She would fill the gaping hole in his life that made him so reticent. They would have children, many, many children and prosper and be respected. She was to be the new matriarch in this dynasty so special that it had its own and single god. She quailed a little at the idea. Surely many gods were safer, there would always be one to appeal to if the others turned against you; to be the focus of a single god was to be completely at his mercy. Though if he were really all-powerful, nothing would be beyond him. Well, it would be worth pleasing such a god. And one day, they might make a visit home and show her brother what she had made of her life. Or perhaps she wouldn't bother.

The next morning after he had breakfasted, Eliezer begged leave to take Rebekah and make his way back to her waiting bridegroom. Laban looked doubtful.

'Hold on. Why don't you let Rebekah stay with us for a while? We will send her to you in good time.'

Eliezer had already understood the depths of Laban's greed.

'My master is very old. He wants to see his son settled.'

'Why don't we ask Rebekah what she wants to do?'

They called her, and Laban, giving her several meaningful looks with his back turned to Eliezer suggested she remain with them for a while longer. Rebekah saw clearly what was on her brother's mind. Why release this goldmine immediately to the eager family? Who knew if there might not be more gifts forthcoming to persuade a reluctant bride to make the journey?

'I am packed and ready to go. I will leave with Eliezer this morning,' Rebekah said coldly.

Laban's eyes dimmed as he saw his plan come to nothing.

'Well, then go.'

And Rebekah took her place in the caravan, along with the nurse who had brought her up, and they headed off south to the new land and the new family that were to become her real life.

Seated outside her husband's tent so many decades later, Rebekah let out a bitter laugh. Her real life. Yes, it had been that. Her real and only life. She recollected the quality of the excitement she felt and how it had built during those camel-riding days as she got closer and closer to her destiny. And as she remembered, the weight bore down on her of the passing years that found her the way she was now, heavy bodied, heavy hearted – what she had known she must become in a flash of foreknowledge at the first glimpse of her betrothed. Was that journey south the last time she had smiled for no reason other than the sheer pleasure of being alive?

They received word that Abraham had died while they were

journeying and that Isaac had gone to Beer-lahai-roi in the Negev desert. Eliezer mourned quietly, but was unsurprised that his master had not survived to meet his daughter-in-law.

'You were his last wish. He was ready.'

'But why has Isaac gone to this other place? Is it permanent?'

Eliezer shook his head. But it was clear the place meant something to him.

'It's a strange name: *The Well of the Living One Who Sees Me*. Who named it?'

'It was a long time ago. Before Isaac was born. It's in the past.'

So they continued south beyond Hebron towards the desert.

The light was beginning to die as they approached their destination. As they passed by open fields on the outskirts of Beer-lahai-roi, Rebekah saw a figure walking towards their caravan. He was not intentionally making for them. He appeared to have no intention at all. He wandered it seemed for movement's sake alone, with his head bowed, his hands limp at his sides. He was perhaps thinking profoundly, or not at all. He was meditating, or praying, or pondering a problem deeply, or just pacing blindly though the open country without a thought in his head, ignoring the world around him, in a dream or in a blank absent-minded daze. It was impossible to say.

'Who is that?' Rebekah asked Eliezer.

'My master. Isaac, the son of Abraham.'

For the sake of custom, Rebekah covered her face, but the gesture secured her a moment of privacy while she took in her husband-to-be. The impossibility of deciding his mood as he walked disturbed Rebekah. It was not the distance between them, but something indistinct about his manner, about his very being, that prevented her from getting any insight into the quality of mind of the man she was going to marry. And with that indistinctness came her only actual sense of him; that he was entirely without energy. Whatever he was doing on his walk, there was a lethargy about the manner in which he barely lifted his limbs and made his way through the landscape, eyes cast down, as if everything that was not him – the earth, the birds singing at the sunset, the very air – effaced him. Eliezer had described him as quiet and hesitant. What Rebekah saw was more – or rather less – than that. She saw a man already defeated. For the first time, she wondered if her new life would be a good one. Before this moment, the thought had not occurred to her.

Rebekah's recollections were interrupted by the arrival of her eldest son. Esau, her rough and ready boy, her savage throwback to – what?

'He wants to see me?'

He was panting from the speed at which he had come run-ning, sweating with the effort and with anxiety and eagerness at having been summoned.

'He wants to see you.'

Rebekah didn't look up at her gasping, worried son.

'What for?'

'Why don't you go in and ask him?'

'But why's he called for me, Ma?'

Rebekah closed her eyes wearily.

'I expect he will tell you if you go in to him. Just *go in*. He's waiting.'

Esau, red-faced and flustered, stared at her for a moment, and then turned towards the opening of the tent. Rebekah con-tinued to sit in the growing heat of the morning sun. There was one thing. Jacob. Her beautiful, clever boy. Jacob was what she had to show for her life.

He had been killed that day. The flash of the blade – but his eyes were blinded with tears and terror? – even now at unexpected moments, that searing light of sun on metal illuminated the interior of his mind. A sudden polished silvery brightness lit up his present darkness, his actual present blindness, but even before his eyes had failed completely, the flash of the blade would blot out what his eyes could see, so that he actually flinched against the expected blow of that day long ago, the blow that never fell. Had not yet fallen. But the moment and eternity of waiting, before it was clear that the cleaver was not going to slice his beating heart in two, murdered Isaac quite as effectively as if it had been driven deep into his flesh. The sight, the thought, the ineradicable knowledge of his father with his arm raised, holding the tool that had become a weapon, preparing to execute his son, killed Isaac, sucked the soul and spirit out of him, leeched him of all substance, bled him to death.

When the blow failed to happen, Isaac waited for a word. But none came. None directed at him. He heard his father say, 'Here I am' yet again, but not to him this time. Then to whom? Isaac had not called his name, his tongue as paralysed as his eyes were blinded. Then he heard the sound of his salvation: the bleating of a sheep. Isaac was not to be sacrificed to his father's jealous god, after all. A sheep would do, it turned out. But not, apparently, until the jealous god was satisfied that his acolyte would have taken obedience as far as it was possible to go. Abraham did not kill his son. But he would have. What other possible interpretation could the boy – or the Lord – have made?

27

After all, Abraham had already shown himself prepared to sacrifice a son. He had expelled Isaac's half-brother and Hagar, his mother, to wander in the deadly Negev. Isaac understood Ishmael to be the bad brother, and he the good one. It was clear then that being a child of the father did not as such save a son. But he had imagined that being a good son, *the* good son, the promise fulfilled, the longed for product of his mother and father together, their hope of future, would keep him safe from what a father could do to his child. That day on Mount Moriah he learned differently. Any son might be sacrificed to the demands of an invisible inaudible voice. The invisible inaudible voice could be more powerful than any ties of the heart or mind, more powerful even than the reason for hearing the voice in the first place – the terrible fact and fear of extinction. Isaac had never heard that voice, but he learned that nothing was more important than its compelling demands.

So a sheep died that day instead. But Isaac did not survive. Certainly, Abraham treated him as if he were dead. He untied his son without a word and proceeded to make a sacrifice of the sheep. Then he turned aside from the place and walked back the way the two of them had come. Isaac followed, limp and shuddering with shock. Abraham said nothing, not a syllable, as he walked back at a faster pace than his shattered son could manage to the lads waiting with the donkey. Isaac trailed behind, but Abraham never turned round to see if he was there. The silence of the journey there was now the silence of their return, but it was a deadlier silence. A silence for lack of words. As if language itself had died up there on Mount Moriah. It was not only Isaac who understood that he had, in fact, been killed. His continued existence was invisible or unbearable to his father. Very likely, both.

The lads too were silenced when they saw Abraham and his son straggling behind. Isaac could not tell what they saw in his father's face, which remained turned away from him, and he couldn't imagine what his own face expressed, but the lads were wide-eyed with wonder at the sight of them and got up without a word, without a glance towards each other, and walked back the way they had come ahead of their master in a fearful speechlessness.

In three days they came to the outskirts of Beer-sheeba where Sarah waited for her family to return from their hunting trip to their home in the glade of tamarisk trees by the well that Abraham had dug long ago. Where they had feasted at the birth of their son. Abraham stood for a moment, and then, without turning back to look at Isaac, he walked steadily, unwaveringly towards the courtyard of the house, and on, without pausing, to his room, which he entered, closing the door behind him. Isaac followed as far as the closed door and then stopped to stare at it for a moment before walking on beyond it towards his mother's room.

Sarah's smile of welcome collapsed into terror at the sight of her son. The silence in the house howled like a wilderness as Isaac stood in front of his mother – a wraith, a pale, shivering ghost, transparent almost, like water, with eyes dim and milky like a blind man.

'What has he done?' Sarah wailed, holding her arms out to Isaac.

'He sacrificed me to his Lord.'

But though that was what Isaac thought he spoke, no words reached Sarah. She only saw his mouth working, straining to speak but achieving nothing, merely a gasping silence. She did not need the words, she saw enough of what Isaac wanted to tell her just by looking at her son. She laid him down in her bed and bathed away the beads of sweat that rolled down his face with cool water, and soothed his trembling body with her stroking hand. Finally, Isaac slept, and when he woke, he told her in his new, parched voice of what had occurred on the mountain in Moriah.

And then there was a sound such as no one had heard ever before. People stopped what they were doing, stopped breathing even, as three long, languishing notes rang out and seemed to still the very air around Beer-sheeba, so that the howl of loss that is the way of the world could be heard to the ends of the earth and at the very edges of time.

Silence fell again like a weighty curtain and that day Sarah took herself away to Kiriath-arba, which is Hebron, in the land of Canaan, leaving the future behind her with the past that was Abraham. And with her went Isaac, the son, the posterity, all that remained of the great complexity of love between Abraham and Sarah.

The death that was implied in Sarah's terrible cries came soon. It was postponed just long enough to put a distance, across which no words could be spoken, between herself and the man who had been her brother, her husband, her lifelong love, and to take her son with her. She died of grief, of despair, of the final unavoidable necessity to confront the way of the world. She gave up. At last she had had enough. She took to her bed in her tent at Hebron and waited to die, tears falling unbidden down her old face, passionless and wanting nothing but nothing more.

And Isaac, the beloved, longed for, cherished child, was left alone. Orphaned. Deserted by both parents. Still too young to let the actual life seep out of him as his mother had, yet too horrorstruck to let any further life in. He left Hebron at the news that Abraham was arriving to arrange Sarah's burial. It was not anger, exactly – Isaac had no access to anger – but something more like a fear of a terrible embarrassment – his father's and his own – if they should meet again over the body of his mother. And it turned out that Abraham had business as well as burial to do in Hebron. He begged the owner of the cave of Machpelah to sell it to him as a burial site, but somehow, rich and powerful as he was, he ended up purchasing the sizeable field which contained the cave. Sarah was buried in the cave, and with the surrounding field the descendants of Abraham had gained a legal foothold in Canaan. Odd, you might think, that Abraham had been obliged to buy a plot of land here for the family, when the Lord had promised it all to him. But Abraham by now knew better than to put all his trust in the promises of his Lord. He had learned that he had to meet his Lord more than halfway; better buy some land than just wait for the Lord to get round to keeping his promises. Abraham knew from bitter experience how long the gifts of the Lord could be in coming, and how far short they might fall when they did eventually come.

Travelling south to avoid his father, Isaac bypassed Beer-sheeba and continued on until, as though that was what he intended all along, he came to Beer-lahai-roi, where he stopped and decided to spend some time. That name – *The Well of the Living One Who Sees Me* – had lingered at the back of his mind and came fresh to him now. Beer-lahai-roi was Hagar's well. It was the place where Hagar and Ishmael, Isaac's half-brother, ran out of the paltry bread and water donated to them by Abraham – a fatherly gesture, indeed – when Sarah, now having a child of her own, forced them into exile in the wilderness.

Where even Abraham's pitiless Lord took pity on their cries of thirst and despair, and struck a well for them and promised that Ishmael would endure as a wild man of the desert. A hunter, a survivor, the father of survivors for generations to come; but always an outcast of the family which had been completed with Isaac and had no further use for the concubine's son. Dim-eyed Isaac saw him now with his inner eye: his brother, the hunter, the wild boy, dark and strong, frightening and wonderful. Beloved and dangerous. Godlike and lethal. *Ishmael*. The name sent thrills of fear and admiration down old Isaac's spine, even after the lifetime that had passed.

'You . . . you . . . c-c-c-called for me, Fa-fa-father?'

Esau stammered when he was nervous. A man desperately ill at ease with words.

'Esau, my son.'

Isaac blindly beckoned to his son, relieved to be brought back to the present, even if the present did mean the end. He sniffed the air. His son had brought the smell of wood smoke and sweat into the tent. Isaac, who saw so little, and feared so much, loved strong smells.

'Here, sit beside me, so I can talk. My voice is weak like the rest of me. Help me sit up better.'

Esau pulled his father forward and fumbled with the pillows behind him. Resting back, Isaac winced; the arrangement of the pillows was all wrong. He was more uncomfortable. He groaned, but said nothing as Esau squatted down beside his father's bed.

'I am old,' Isaac began in a quavering voice.

'Not s-s-so old, F-f—'

Isaac waved the interruption aside.

'I am old,' he insisted more firmly, not to be denied his tragedy. 'Grown old and already blind and sick for so long. I could die at any time. It will be soon.'

Esau made a sound that was strangled by his father's impatient shushing. But he reached out for Esau's huge hairy hand and stroked it as if he were appreciating the finest polished wood.

'I'd like a little treat. For an old dying man. You know how I love a good strong gamey stew. My mouth's watering for powerful flavours. Go out and trap something tasty for me and make me a stew this one last time, my son, my wild, hunting son, and then I'll give you my final blessing before I die.'

Esau beamed at his father's demand of him and clutched the frail, bony hand that stroked his. His stammer disappeared, leaving just the coarse, country accent he had picked up from his unruly boyhood and manhood days amid the local Canaanites.

'Yeah, I'll go and catch something and cook it just like you like it. But don't talk about dying. You let me bring you something really tasty, and tomorrow I'll bring more, and the next day for years and years . . .'

'I must give you my blessing, Esau. There won't *be* years and years. You are my successor by birthright as the oldest, and also in my love. It has to be pronounced before the Lord of Abraham.'

Esau stood massive over his feeble father and bent down to plant a scratchy bearded kiss on Isaac's pale sagging cheek.

'Back soon. You just wait and see what I'll bring you.'

'Don't be too long,' Isaac croaked, raising up his quivering hand to stroke the roughness of his son's face. 'I don't have much time.'

33

Tears sprang to Esau's eyes, dampening the thick red eye-lashes.

'P-p-please, Fa-fa-fa-fa—'

But the old man waved his objections away, so he turned and hurried out of the tent.

The bench outside Isaac's tent was empty, though Esau was too preoccupied with thoughts of the hunt to notice. Rebekah returned to her own tent as fast as her heavy old body and her pain would allow her when she heard what her husband wanted of their older son. Jacob was sitting at the table chewing dream-ily on bread and honey. He looked up as Rebekah entered.

'So, Mother, what was so urgent with Father this time? Here, come and sit down and finish your breakfast.'

Rebekah sat but did not eat.

'We've got to do something. He's going to give his blessing to Esau. He says he's dying.'

'He always says he's dying. Anyway, it doesn't matter, Esau's already given me his birthright. Whatever he inherits is mine. He exchanged it for a bowl of lentil stew.'

'What?'

Jacob shook his head at the memory of the idiocy of his older brother.

'A few months back. He came in from a hunt, oh, in such a state. Sweating like an ox, grunting, an animal, you know how he gets after a chase, like one of the beasts he's been hunting down. He hadn't caught anything. He'd been out all day, stalk-ing and pouncing and whatever he does in the wilderness and got absolutely nothing for his pains. He was in tears like a kid, snuffling, when he came past my tent. I had just made some lentil stew – the way you showed me – for . . . well, for father.

You know how he likes his food, and Esau for bringing it to him. I thought if I . . . that he might . . .' Jacob lifted his shoulders and let it go.. 'So Esau charged in to my tent and grunted at me. "Gimme some of that red stuff you got there . . ." As articulate as ever, my oafish brother. He stared at the stew as if it were water in the desert, as if it were life itself. "I'm starved," he growled. So I put some in a bowl and held it out to him, though before he could take it I snatched it back. "Sell me your birthright," I said. He didn't get it for a moment. "Give it me," he grunted. But I kept it out of his reach. "Sell me your birthright, older brother." So he shrugged. "I'm dying of hunger. What good's a birthright to me if I'm dead of starvation? I want my belly full." "So you will?" I asked, and said he had to swear, and he did. "So your birthright is now mine," I said. He nodded, "Yeah, yeah," and snatched the bowl and slurped it down in a second, then he had another, and then more, until he had eaten the lot. He even looked grateful to me as he left. So it doesn't matter if father gives him his blessing, it's mine.'

Rebekah looked disbelievingly at Jacob.

'And you're supposed to be my clever son,' she said dropping her head into her hands, wearily. 'You're crafty, you think fast, but you don't understand the world at all. All those years of school-learning and scroll-studying have given you great knowledge about laws and none about life. Do you think such a promise will stand? Have you got anything in writing? Esau's mark on a piece of paper? What do you think your little trick adds up to compared to a father's dying blessing? The trouble is you aren't tricky enough, Jacob. You trust that once you have done your dubious deal with the world, the world will honour it. It's not only fools who are fools. Why shouldn't Esau just laugh

35

in your face once Isaac is dead? Promise or no promise? He'll be the one with the blessing, the oldest son with the birthright, whatever he swore in private to you. Do you want Esau to inherit everything? Do you think he's fit to head this household, to maintain our land and our power? Do you think just because he's not as clever as you that he will hand it all over to you? "Oh yes, Jacob, you're much cleverer than me, you had better have everything." What did I do that both my sons should be idiots?'

Rebekah slapped her forehead with her palms. Jacob frowned at his mother.

'Well, morally the birthright is mine. Esau values the satisfaction of a moment's hunger more than his inheritance. Of course, I'm better suited to taking over, but Father won't see it. Why won't he see it? All he understands is . . . what? Esau's game stew in his mouth. He loves Esau. Nothing I've done has made him love me.'

Rebekah relented and reached out to stroke Jacob's fine dark hair.

'Everything you've done has made *me* love you. You're my clever, beautiful son. And if you'd done nothing I'd still love you. I love you because I love you. Because I look at you and my heart aches with love. You are your grandfather Abraham's child. That was the man I should have married. I never met him, but I knew my time was wrong. Instead, I got . . . Your father is like Esau. A coarse, greedy man whose only interest is in appeasing his appetite. Give him what he can taste or feel or smell and he's happy for a moment. Nothing else touches him. He's an empty fool, and always has been.'

'Well, fool or not, I can't stop Father from blessing Esau, can I?'

36

'Listen to me. We will do something about it. Go out to our flocks and bring me two fine kids. I'll cook them just the way your father likes. I'll make him such a stew. He won't know it's not wild game by the time I've finished with it. You'll take it to him, let him eat and when he's full to bursting he will give you his dying blessing. He's blind, he won't know you're not Esau.'

'Oh Mother,' Jacob laughed. 'Esau's nearly as hairy as a goat himself, and I'm your smooth-skinned boy. Father has only got to touch me and he'll know I'm not Esau. If he realises I'm cheating him he won't give me his blessing, he'll curse me and all my offspring.'

Rebekah smiled.

'So your objection to cheating your father is merely practical? You don't mind tricking him so long as you don't get caught?'

Jacob winced. He was alarmed by the truth of that, but he adjusted rapidly.

'I tricked Esau, why not my father? It's stupid that Esau should inherit everything just because he's a moment older than me and because he brings Father game. But I don't think it can be done. Isaac isn't blind enough for that. He'll guess it's me and I'll lose everything.'

'Don't worry about the curses. I'll take them on myself. And I'll take care of the problems. Just hurry up and get the kids.'

When Jacob returned with the dead kids, she skinned and prepared them. While they were cooking, she fetched some of Esau's clothes and brought them back to her tent.

'Put these on.'

'But he's blind.'

'He can smell, can't he? And you smell far too sweet to be Esau just back from the hunt.'

She cut lengths of the goat skins from the kids she had

cooked and tied them over Jacob's hands and wrists and around his neck.

'And he can feel.'

'But even Esau doesn't feel like a goat.'

'My son, when people want things very badly, you'd be surprised how easily satisfied with approximations they are. And sometimes people think they want something when they know better. Isaac loves Esau, but he can't really believe that Esau would be the best of his sons to inherit. So give him an opportunity to make a mistake. You are my cleverest son, and I love you as much as my own life. You have many gifts, but you understand nothing about people. Jacob, the years have given me very little, mostly they've taken everything away – except knowledge about people. You are all I've got, all I love, all that matters. Do this for me. And for you. Let's not waste my life entirely.'

She handed the steaming spicy goat stew and fresh baked bread to Jacob. And disguised against scent and touch, he took it to his blind father.

Rebekah watched Jacob leave and hoped it was true what she said about people wanting things so badly they took what they were offered and believed they had what they wanted. She knew it hadn't been true for her. If only she had had such blindness. What she had wanted all those years ago, when she was a waiting girl, she had wanted as passionately as it was possible to feel. But had there been a single moment, after the camel journey, when she felt she had what she dreamed of for herself? Her heart had sunk at the sight of the pallid boy she saw in the distance who she was told was her future. Quiet, needing to be brought out of himself, Eliezer had said. And she might have believed that as, behind her veil, she watched him walk towards her. He could have been fecund with latent character and vigour, but something in her understood he wasn't. Far from containing promise, she saw the Isaac who was to be her husband as already lost. What it was about him that told her this, she couldn't say. Something about the way he walked, his arms limp, his head hung, but more than that, it was as if he were enclosed in a grey gossamer shroud, something that made him hazy and indistinct in the world even as he came more clearly into view. She saw him better and she saw nothing. A body that seemed to have no boundaries, to lack a solid edge between itself and the world. An amorphous image that went, once she saw them, with the lost, undefined look in his eyes. Her husband. A wraith. A barely there man as frail in his existence as water pouring into the sand from an upturned jug. Her new life.

He was in mourning, of course, for his father, and his mother was already dead. A man newly orphaned. She tried to remember that as she stepped down and was introduced to her bridegroom by Eliezer who explained to Isaac what Abraham had asked him to do before he had died. Explained? Who was this grown man whose marriage was arranged without his knowledge or participation? Isaac nodded his understanding or his agreement, it wasn't clear which. Then he looked at Rebekah. Even behind her veil it was obvious she was a lovely young woman. His narrowing eyes showed her that he could see that. At last, a real expression passed over his face. A covert gaze under lowered lids, piercing and sullen, while behind the depths of the occluded pupils equally clouded thought lay. She had seen this look on the faces of young men when she passed them on the streets of Haran. A wily, dangerous half-lidded look from a body as still and concentrated as a statue. Those anonymous seconds had caused Rebekah to shiver apprehension while, safely chaperoned, she learned to flicker a look of her own before she passed the young men by. It was a game, but there was, in the deepest place of their gaze, something deadly and hungrily serious that disturbed even the youthful Rebekah's confidence. Now, seeing it just fleetingly again on her betrothed, Rebekah shuddered, even though, slight and a little stringy as he was, Isaac was a handsome enough young man. This was a passing look that she could not pass by. The eyes that gazed at her were those of the man she had agreed to marry, sight unseen. The look of the stranger would become the regard of her husband, the father of her children. The first terrible panic welled up in her as she understood absolutely that she had no more options to take. There was neither going back nor going forward. She was where she would be for the rest of her life.

Isaac returned to Hebron where his mother had chosen to die, with his bride-to-be.

A few days after she had arrived, he came to her one morning.

'Please, come with me . . .' He spoke urgently, stammering his request.

She followed him, not altogether willingly. He led her to the tent where he ate and slept. When she lingered in the opening, reluctant to enter alone with a man she had not yet married, he took her hand and pulled her inside, like a child brooking no hesitation.

'This was where my mother died,' he told her, leading her to the back of the tent. 'That was the bed she lay on waiting to be taken. It's my bed now. My mother loved me, I think. But once she got here, she lay down on that bed and let herself die. Then

40

I had no one. But now, there is you. Let's not wait long to get married.'

'But your father . . . you're still in mourning . . .'

He shook his head firmly.

'No, I don't mean the wedding. Be my wife. Understand? I want a *wife*.'

His eyes clouded over as that look came over his face again. It seemed to Rebekah that he was not seeing her any more, and yet even as his focus went vague his hands reached for her breasts, and a small moan ran like a shiver up his body until it caught in his throat as he clutched at them beneath the cloth, clawing at their fullness. When she tried to pull away in fright, he tightened his hold on each breast and used them to drag her nearer to his body. With his face so close to hers that she could feel the moisture of his breath through her veil, he spoke in a strangled whine.

'I've never had a woman. I've dreamed about them. My brother told me about them, but he laughed and said I'd never get a decent one of my own. But you are beautiful. Now I need you, I've been alone and I need you . . .'

'We're not married,' Rebekah whispered, terrified to raise her voice in case someone might find them.

'We're betrothed. I want you now. Don't argue, you're my wife. You will be.'

And all the time he pulled at the opening of her robe until finally it ripped and his hands reached inside to take the actual flesh of her breasts into his grasp and squeeze them until she cried out in pain.

'Please, please, don't.'

'Shh, be quiet,' he hissed.

'You're hurting me,' she insisted sharply. 'Let me go.'

'Huh?' He was faintly surprised at her protestations. Ridiculous when they were practically married. But there was no stopping to make conversation. He let go one breast, still pumping and kneading at the other, and reached down towards her belly and beyond to find an oasis of wiry hair and then the gap he made by pushing and pressing his fingers between her legs. Only dreamed about and whispered of by Ishmael. That place. She sobbed shock at his touch, and then cried out as his ignorant hands clumsily explored the textures and layers of her secret flesh. He was nothing but urgent need, blind to everything except the pursuit of his own relief. The imperative was very great and soon Rebekah was on the bed he had been nudging her towards and he had parted her legs and entered her hurriedly, making frenetic movements to release the fury that had built up inside him. After a frantic writhing he gave a caterwaul of triumph, and it was over in a moment, which was something, at least, to be grateful for in the immediate aftermath of her ordeal.

So Rebekah met two husbands before the actual wedding celebrations. One an unfinished outline, a pale shadow, the other an eruption of violent need. A wraith and a rapist in the one person. Here was the beginning of her understanding of the shifting nature of the human species, and here too, simultaneously, was a foretaste of the rest of her life. She was not essentially an innocent girl. She had grasped the meaning of the looks the young men threw at her in Haran. She knew her own power as a young and beautiful woman, she understood how it might be transmuted into a substantial existence as wife and mother. The trade was clear enough when she watched the young men's eyes on her and then looked at the local matriarchs wielding power in the family and the community. The

42

young men looked at these older women with care, though circumspectly, as if they might have seen the ghost of them in the passing pretty young ones, and the spectre of their own youthful power in the strong older women, but were too overwhelmed by desire to understand what it was they were noticing. But in spite of the fun of looking and the wishfulness and the game she and the boys pantomimed delicately on the streets, Rebekah understood the pattern that life was supposed to make. There could be pleasures and delights, and they would be a bonus, but there was also work to be done to make the life you wanted. She was a practical girl, but even so, she had never contemplated the possibility of finding herself with a husband who, though offering her the worldly position she wanted, was himself intolerable. Her youth and optimism had never permitted such a vision. She did not expect to be overwhelmed with love and desire, but she supposed without thinking about it too much that her husband would be quite good enough to get on with.

Now, lying next to her gasping husband-to-be, her clothes torn, her body bruised and painful, wetness seeping between her legs, she contemplated her future with the man who Eliezer had told her needed someone of his own in order to blossom. There were no tears: how could mere tears express her despair and the hopelessness of her situation? There was no escape from this. Isaac was right, she was already his wife, there was no going back once she had left her family. And left with not a moment's hesitation. The possibility that she would become the wife of such a man, this ghost-beast, would not, could not have crossed her mind. But now she lay on the deathbed of her betrothed's mother and understood with every pulse in her body the meaning of bleakness, the end of everything, the prospect of nothing filling a person's life. And the life was hers.

Weep for her.

Isaac had returned to Beer-lahai-roi when his father died. First he and Ishmael buried him next to Sarah in the cave of Machpelah. Ishmael came back for the occasion, dark and strong, his own man, quite other, but the half-brothers had no word for each other and when the job was done Ishmael went off again with nothing more than a nod. So Isaac went to Hagar's well, the place of Ishmael's mother, and sat beside it and dully traipsed the fields around it without any clear sense of what he wanted. Of course, there was one thing he wanted, the one thing he had always wanted: to be Ishmael, to be vivid and bold, not to care, to scorn affection and see the world with a cold, clear eye. But even as a child he knew he would never be that, mostly because Ishmael said he would never be and he believed everything his older brother told him.

'Milksop! Mama's boy! Worm!' Ishmael would chant at the sight of Isaac trailing behind him. 'Do everything you're told. That's the way. Why not suck from your old mother's titties? Gift from the Lord! What a gift.'

Isaac cowered and kept his distance but followed nonetheless. The child was unnaturally good, always wishing to please his elderly parents and seeming to have no will of his own. He was determined only in his devotion to his half-brother. Sometimes Ishmael's rough contempt was exchanged for something else.

'Come here,' Ishmael would jerk his head, giving Isaac permission to come up beside him. 'You're a poor kid.' He would put a brotherly arm around the younger slightly quivering boy.

44

'Don't you want to have fun instead of keeping clean and tidy? You don't know how to have fun, do you?'

Isaac shook his head. He had no idea. He only knew how to be what his parents wanted, to be the late late flowering of their love, to be the proof of his father's faith in himself and his Lord, and the only prospect of the future. Fun, being dirty, going off, being rough was the opposite of those things. Ishmael was the opposite of those things. There was no doubt that their father did not care much for him and that Isaac's mother could hardly bear the sight of him. Isaac could not imagine what it would be like not to be cherished. But Ishmael, it seemed from every indication, *did not care* that he was not loved. He scorned love and was only what he chose to be. He despised love if it meant that he had to be something that he wasn't. He laughed at the caresses Sarah poured on Isaac. Nobody ever kissed Ishmael. Who, indeed, would have dared, even if they had thought of it?

And once, just once, Ishmael had taken Isaac off with him into the wilderness. With his bow and arrows slung across his shoulder, Ishmael led his little brother away from home, or at any rate did not shout at him to go away, stop following him and get back to his mama's lap. Indeed, he even looked behind him from time to time as if to check his follower still followed. Isaac was terrified, repeatedly looking behind him in case he was seen, or perhaps fearing to lose his way back home. Ishmael sneered and told Isaac to keep up, which he tried hard to do though his legs were much shorter and his heart beat thunderously. Ishmael barely spoke to him all during that day, but Isaac watched as his fleet, agile brother stalked his prey and let arrows fly and took his knife and skinned the rabbit he had killed, waving the bloody corpse under his cringing little brother's nose.

'Make a fire.'

Isaac had no idea how to make a fire. Ishmael snorted and got one going. When the rabbit was barely singed he tore off the limbs and stripped them of their meat with his teeth, sucking the bloody juices noisily. He threw scraps to Isaac. Inedible waste, as far as Isaac was concerned, having only eaten the most succulent pieces of meat chosen lovingly for him by his mother. Innards, scrawn. But he ate them because Ishmael told him to, and if his stomach turned at some of the morsels, he also noticed the powerful taste in his mouth, the dark satisfaction on the back of his tongue which suffused through the lining of his cheeks and made his mouth water for more.

They began their return journey as it was growing dark and the shadows made Isaac tremble.

'Scared, little brother? Isn't the world a strange and threatening place when Mummy's out of sight and the light isn't burning all night to keep the monsters away? Ha!'

Isaac tried to hold Ishmael's hand but he shook it off.

'You can hang on to my belt if you must,' he said gruffly.

It was a concession beyond all Isaac's hopes. An acknowledgement of him by his brother. For the first time allowed to touch, to be considered by him.

'Let go of me,' Ishmael brushed Isaac's hand from his belt as soon as they were in sight of the camp. 'Get away from me.'

Isaac straggled, exhausted, into the camp behind his brother who sauntered on not looking back with his hunting trophies slung over his shoulder. Isaac was filthy, his clothes torn, his legs and arms scratched, his face blackened by smoke from the fire, his chin smothered in grease from the fat he had eaten, one eye blackening from where he had fallen over and hit a rock and Ishmael had had to stop and pull him up.

There was a scream. It was not Sarah expressing joy at finding her son after the whole household had been searching most of the day. She ran over to Isaac and shouted at Ishmael.

'What have you done to him?'

Ishmael turned and saw the sorry state of his younger brother. He broke into a laugh.

'He's had a good day. Haven't you, kid?'

Isaac opened his mouth to say he had, the best day of his life, when he looked at his mother's face. He closed his mouth again and said nothing.

The next day Ishmael and his mother left the encampment. Isaac never saw him again until the day they both buried their father.

After his mother died it was to Beer-lahai-roi that Isaac went to avoid his father, to the place where Abraham's Lord saved the life of his half-brother. He didn't know why. If he was in search of lost family, he found nothing. Still he went back again when his father died. Again he found nothing. But ready to return home to Hebron he was presented with a wife chosen for him by his father's servant. His father, it seemed, was never lost. Not even after he had died.

Isaac was comforted in his mother's tent. He lay next to his bride-to-be remembering the sensations that had rushed through his body, still feeling their echo. What a man feels. What Ishmael felt when he had a woman. Alive. A living creature. Not since that day when Ishmael had thrown the disgusting and delicious scraps of wild meat at him had he experienced such pleasure, such vibrancy shooting through his body, so that he actually felt he had a body. Strong flavours, strong sensations were the only counter to his sense of being already dead, already disembodied. Lying there on his mother's bed, he felt, for a little while, vivid as he had not done since before his father had lain him on that altar on Mount Moriah. Isaac grunted his satisfaction, and flung an arm out sideways. It landed on Rebekah's belly and he remembered he was not alone. Turning his head he saw her, dishevelled, her eyes closed. He supposed she was asleep. Now he had a woman, a wife. She would make him food, and provide him with sexual pleasure whenever he wanted. Perhaps, after all, he had found what he was looking for; what he had lost when his mother died – and more. If there was even the shadow of curiosity at whether Rebekah felt as he did, the thought drained away as sleep came over him and completed his rare and delicious sense of well-being.

The war began inside Rebekah and never reached a conclusion. It started at the moment when her husband-to-be laid his coarse, blind hands on her, and it raged in her for the rest of her life. She would never know peace again, not if peace comprised a sense of clarity, a final choice as to how she should proceed in the world of her life. One thing was certain: this *was* to be her life. There would be no escape. Let us be clear on this: such a notion did not and could not have occurred to her. Such a notion was not available. There are times when editors must point out that what-ifs cannot apply, even in the realm of human stories. There was only what her attitude was to be to the life she had been handed, or so hurriedly taken. There could be and always would be only two attitudes: to despair, or to live with and try to improve her lot. Neither option is easy to take, though despair, once embraced, is the easier to sustain. It is difficult initially to give up all hope. The required leap into the absolute black is

terrifying; the attraction of false hope is strong and to acknowledge that an awful reality *is* reality and will be, takes
monumental courage. Nonetheless, once the decision is made,
despair takes care of itself. It feeds on itself and reproduces
itself every moment of every day. There is a certain comfort in
the absolutely negative; there is no need, no point in striving. In
the profoundest, blackest depth of hopelessness there is perpetual pain but no anguish. You can relax into the certainty of
abjection. However, the moment before the plunge is taken,
there is a natural resistance, a foreknowledge that giving up
hope is hopeless. The alternative offers itself: work on the life,
manage it, improve it, wrench it into a more pleasing shape –
and if this turns out to be impossible, then find interior ways of
making it bearable. And understandably, the initial resistance to
this course of action is a vast weariness at the prospect, a reluc-
tance to battle against the unfairness of a bad deal, an attraction
to just giving up and sinking so low that life can pass by over-
head unseen in the cosseting gloom. The resistance to effort is
reasonable because the more positive route doesn't banish either
anguish or the possibility of relapsing into hopelessness when
the terrible weariness of *trying* becomes overwhelming. And
who knows, who will ever know, why one person chooses the
blackness and another the light? Perhaps a youthful over-
optimism and then terrible disappointment is the most likely
route to despair? A little inbuilt uncertainty may save a person
against the shock of life's imperfection. Most people, for
whatever reason, take one or other attitude.

But there are some who never make the choice. They hover
over their options and lurch from one to the other during the
course of their days and become a perpetual internal battle-
ground. This was how it was for Rebekah, who never would

find solace in one thing or the other and who lived in anguish *and* pain, clear-sightedly bleak and hopeless about her prospect, but still attempting occasionally to wrench her life back into something less than intolerable. This also, in his own unthinking way, was how it was for Isaac, dead in spirit, fearful of life and death, but grasping too at whatever seemed physically to enhance the flavour of his life and occasionally, briefly, to overcome the permanent taste and scent of death. Isaac managed to self-indulge the paradox. Rebekah barely survived it.

They were married very soon and quietly in view of the fact that the bridegroom was still in mourning for his father. Rebekah's method of survival in those early days was to make herself the effective head of the household while permitting Isaac to retain the nominal deference due to the man of the family. She had some of what she wanted: wealth and control of daily life. There was no older generation to defer to. Servants and workers learned quickly to come to her for decisions, and she kept Isaac informed, where necessary, of what decisions he was to believe he had made. Her power could only increase: there would be children and grandchildren and she would become the dominating force of the clan she would create. This was something. The creation of the clan would mean that her horror of her husband's touch, her disgust at his physical presence – the way he gorged on food and drink, the way he snatched at her unwilling flesh – would have to be tolerated, at least for a time. But then the misery would overcome her – what she had to put up with in order to get something of what she wanted, and what she would never have – and she would sink into the insufferability of her existence. The result was that she came to everything with bitterness and bad grace. Her way of putting up with the intolerable was to be seen to be putting up with it, and since the existence of the intolerable in her life seeped into even the activities she found gratifying, nothing gave her satisfaction; dissatisfaction became her indelible manner. She put up with the worst things and the finest things. She sighed, bemoaned, complained and shouted. Nothing pleased her, not even what pleased her.

Perhaps if Isaac had not done her such violence so immediately; or perhaps even if, lying beside her, he had noticed her misery and wondered if he had anything to do with it – then she might have seen a possibility of trying to show her husband other ways to be a man. He might have learned about pleasure rather than mere satisfaction, about the sensual possibilities of delicacy and deferment when the other is a willing partner. Probably, he would not. Isaac, having found a few gross satisfactions in his pale life, would likely not have given them up for something subtler. But Rebekah did not try – even in her determined moments – to find a way to overcome her physical revulsion. She observed the onset of his greed – for food or for her – with careful intensity, positively stoking the fire of her disgust.

'Bring me food. Tasty food . . . Come here. Get your clothes off.'

His eyes would glaze, sometimes she would even see saliva at the corners of his mouth. The gluttonous leer she saw in the first moment of their meeting appeared again, whether he hungered for food or sex. And she focused on it, gazing at the lubricity that seeped even from the pores of his pallid sweaty flesh; punishing him with her vision of him, and punishing herself too. And in between, he complained in the high-pitched

51

whine of one who cannot fathom what exactly is wrong and doesn't care to know why.

'I'm sick. Too ill to get out of bed today. I feel weak. I'm dying. My legs, my head, my arms, my chest . . . Bring me medicine. Make me more comfortable. I can't breathe, I can't sleep, I can't walk, I can't speak to anyone. I can't see. My eyes hurt – oh, it's as if knives are being twisted in them. It's always dark. It's getting darker . . . help me . . . I'm too cold . . . too hot. My bowels . . . my belly . . . oh, my heart . . .'

All the medicine that skilled healers could come up with did nothing for his ailments, nothing worked, nothing made him feel he might survive the approaching day or night – except the strong taste of food in his mouth or a pliant breast under his grasping fingers and the pounding of his thighs against Rebekah's soft flesh in his desperate efforts to shudder away the pressure between his loins. And no sooner had the taste faded and the relief become no more than memory, than all that ailed him and all that would forever ail him returned to torment him once again.

In their old age Rebekah received his complaints in cold silence or harsh sarcasm. She arranged his bedding, lightened or added to his clothing, provided remedies, did whatever was demanded, but always icily, always giving nothing, making her contempt clear.

'I think I'm dying.'

'How fortunate for you. I wish I could get out of this existence early.'

'The pain is terrible, I can't bear it, give me poison to end it.'

'Certainly. Take some for me too.'

'I'm shivering. I can't stop shivering.'

Just a shrug and the blanket pulled roughly under his chin.

'No, no, shivering with fever.'

Another shrug and the blanket whisked away.

'Well?'

'Well, stay with me.'

'Is that what you want?'

'I don't want to be alone.'

'Oh, we're all alone. Are you ordering me to stay with you, as my husband?'

A look of confusion. What he wants. He can't put his finger on it. Not alone. But someone to stroke . . . to care . . . He shakes his head.

'No.'

Sometimes he nods.

'Yes.'

She leaves or she stays. Nothing is improved.

So she was with him in the later years. But more often in the early days, the despair welled up inside her and she screamed her misery and dissatisfaction out loud at him. Did it mean she still had a glimmer of hope that things might change? Or perhaps, being younger and closer to the shock of her reality, she was simply unable to control herself. She would scream to him, or no one in particular, increasingly out of control.

'I hate my life. Why, why, why did it have to be you? Get up. Be half a man. See to this, why do I have to do everything? If only I'd never been born. This terrible punishment. The gods hate me. Your Lord hates me. But why? Why? If only I'd stayed where I was. Oh, someone, some god, something, help me, help me, help me . . .'

She wailed and shrieked at him and at anyone who demanded anything of her in those moments when intolerability rose up in her gorge like vomit. People quailed, never knowing what response they would receive to the most reasonable requests.

Isaac writhed with misery under her tongue, too helpless even to understand why she complained to him, let alone offer anything that might placate her. Her rage exploded doubly at his lack of response. Everyone feared her outbursts, but neither was she liked when she was under control with her pinched mouth and snapping tone. She did not ask to be liked. She was absorbed entirely in the drama of the battle within herself: the terrible oscillation that demanded she take control of her miserable circumstances, or give up doing anything, and resulted in nothing but her need to howl her resentment at whoever dared to interrupt her misery.

But when the lust rose in Isaac, in those early years, often and often though it was, she always kept herself firmly under control. Here would be the only sense her life could now make. Only through her disgust would anything emerge that made her life acceptable. Offspring, children, a family of her own was the only hope, and the only way to them was through the loathsome touch of her husband. When she had secured a dynasty she would be able to control it. The children would be hers – what authority could Isaac possibly have? The future would be hers and if she was to be denied happiness she could at least be in charge of posterity. So again and again she supported the weight of his frantic thrashing body, the pain of his stupid greedy hands, his vile grunts and snorting satisfaction. She did her wifely duty whenever it was required, but after, when it was over, she sent her servants for hot water and scrubbed Isaac off every part of her, her disgust growing deeper, her flesh shuddering and building layers of insensitivity at the memory of his touch. When enough children were born, she would find him a concubine – some poor girl who had even less choice in her life than she – and at last be free from his grasp. Until then she swallowed bile and tried to keep her face at least impassive and her mind blank when he approached.

And yet, the children failed to come. Month after month she retired to the women's tent, relieved at the brief respite from Isaac's attentions but aware that again no child had been made. She knew, of course, of Sarah and Abraham's difficulty in producing offspring, how Isaac was the child of their old age. Barren was a word that began to enter her thoughts. Was she, like Sarah, barren? It was unthinkable for a year or so, because to accept it was to give up all chance of making her life in any degree tolerable. To live *this* life and have nothing of her own ever was not to be thought about – she was so young, the years so long. But eventually as the years began to mount up and nothing happened, even her terror of the truth could not conceal it from her. Was there to be nothing good in her life ever? Was it really possible that she who had been so young and with so much hope and trust in the future might have an entire lifetime of emptiness without any consolation? Was this to be the totality of her actual life? It began to seem that it was.

'What, exactly, was the point of all those promises that precious Lord made to your father if I don't conceive?' she shouted at Isaac, nagging him, as if he were responsible for the Lord's oversight instead of, as ever, the victim of His whims.

Isaac had no answer.

'Haven't you suffered enough at the hands of your father's Lord? It's not enough he demanded your blood, and turned you into a quivering old man before your time, now he prevents you having children. He's a trickster, your Lord. Or else he finds you as anaemic as I do and has gone off to find a better prospect. What is the point of you if you don't make children?'

And Isaac had no answer.

Rebekah's complaints about her empty life, loud and vivid though they were, washed over Isaac for the most part. While she railed and screamed, he thought about his next meal, his last copulation and whatever it was that pained or distressed him that day. Sometimes he just turned over in his bed and slept or nodded off at the table after he had finished eating, even while she was berating him. But one complaint he couldn't easily ignore; her barrenness was not hers alone. Her questions broke through the distractions of his continual present and made themselves heard all too well. What *was* the point of him? Why had he had to suffer that terrible, blinding sight of his father raising the cleaver above his head if he was to be the end of the line? These were not questions he asked himself as the childless years went by, they were questions he shied away from at all costs. But an angry, disappointed wife knows exactly the questions that most need to be evaded, and most need to be asked.

He was his father's chosen son. The child his Lord had promised. Isaac was promise fulfilled: the outcome of his extraordinary father's faith in a new alliance between one man and the invisible world. Isaac was laughter, the rush of joy at the arrival of proof. And yet, Isaac was not Abraham, the boy was not the father. The proof had been no more than proof of the quality of the father. When had Abraham's Lord ever made himself known to Isaac, the son? Not a word, not a whisper, not an intimation. What promises had Isaac been given? There was no alliance, no declaration of love, no ritual covenant for him. All Isaac knew of the invisible world was silence. Yet who else could continue Abraham's line? He was the only one with his father's blessing, the only one who had been spoken of as the continuation by the Lord. So where were *his* children? The years had passed. No word, no promise and no children. And Isaac knew perfectly well why. *He was not his father.* How could he be? His father had killed him. The Lord had killed him. He was nothing. Just a term between two powerful wills. A negotiating point. Between them he had been negated. The only hope of the tribe of Abraham and yet no hope at all.

With the incessant encouragement of Rebekah, he finally dared to apply to the God of Abraham for an answer to the question of posterity. God would not speak to him, but at the insistence of his wife he risked a petition to the Lord at the altar built by his father, and reminded Him of his covenant with Abraham, tremulously nagging the Lord as Isaac was nagged about the absence of future. There was, after all, a promise to be kept. And the Lord heard, it seemed. The Lord heard and the Lord at long last caused Rebekah to conceive.

After so long. But if in the earliest days of her pregnancy it seemed that the Lord had remembered his responsibilities and was belatedly making up for his neglect, Rebekah very soon began to wonder whether disturbing this tricky God with petitions had resulted not in answered prayers but in retribution for bothering him. The complexity of the newfangled notion of an all-powerful personal god became clearer to her as the pregnancy developed. The relationship between an individual and his Lord, she learned, was as unreliable and erratic as it was between man and wife or father and son. Just as the absence of her monthly bleeding began to persuade her that this personal god actually existed, she had cause to wonder whether that was, after all, such a good thing, if as well as powerful he was also capricious. Better surely to have the formal relations her family had had with their more distant gods and rely on their multiplicity to even out any unfairnesses, than risk getting exactly what you want only to discover that it was punishment. Who, with just this single omnipotent god, was there to turn to in complaint?

As the pregnancy progressed it began to seem as if the battle Rebekah had long experienced in her mind between acceptance and despair of her lot was now being played out by actual warring forces within her body. Her swollen belly heaved with growing discontentment. Though she longed for sleep, there was no rest, day or night, not a moment when she closed her eyes without the pain wrenching her awake again. While other women smiled with pleasure at the feel of their child quickening within them, she suffered agonies from an unending turmoil of writhing and kicking inside the prison of her flesh. Her eyes darkened into hollowed-out pits with exhaustion and pain, but there was never any relief. The battle inside her didn't let up. She became convinced that whatever was growing in her was filled with venom and hatred, tormenting her for imprisoning it, fighting to escape, pummelling her sore and aching body with rage when it failed. She lived in terror of it, convinced that it would kill her before she could get free of it, that she would die of sleep-deprivation and physical agony, or worse, that it would consume her insides away, or rip her belly open in a final desperate bid for freedom. She wept as the sun rose and as the sun set and all the hours in between, and she screamed at Isaac for being the cause of such misery, threatening to cut the dreadful thing out of her, to destroy herself rather than put up with such suffering. The escape of childbearing turned out to be a poisonous chimera, just like her marriage had been. Only a woman cursed could have such intolerable luck. But what had she done? The old question. How could she possibly have deserved this terrible existence? She had only ever been young and innocent before the misery of her destiny befell her. What possible crime or sin could she have committed to deserve such an existence?

'I'd rather die. I won't live through this. I can't survive it. Your monster inside me is killing me. Why is this happening to me?' she screamed over and over at Isaac.

But Isaac had no answer.

'Do something for once in your life. I've been cursed by your wretched god. What have I done to him? You got me into this. Tell him to stop punishing me.'

But it was clear that no matter how miserable Isaac might be, he was not about to complain to his dangerously powerful god about getting what he had petitioned him for.

'Then *I* will.'

Isaac gaped.

'You can't.'

'I'm not afraid of your god. What could happen that would be worse than this?'

'You have to do what he . . . you have to put up with . . . the Lord is . . .'

But she was already on her way, dragging her struggling burden and swollen legs to the altar to put her case to the God of Abraham.

She howled her deep sense of injustice at the Lord just as she howled at Isaac.

'So tell me. Why? Why . . . why me . . . why . . .?'

But words, like life, failed her.

*

It was not a monster that she carried, but two monstrous unborn wills, each striving for space in their confinement, each determined to prevail, and, when the time came, reach the light the other threatened to obscure. Two single, separate forces battled blindly for life against an unknown but palpable obstacle, against an unknowable other, against not-self. Two strangers, knowing nothing of each other but obstruction, fought against proximity and the gross accident of multiplicity. Only singleness would do for each of them. Only everything was enough. The battle for omnipotence, for the totality of existence was unceasing during all the months of gestation. It was a true struggle for existence. And the battle continued even as they suffered the agony of expulsion into the world. As each great wave of pressure impelled them forward, they wrestled for primacy; each jostling to be the first to take in the light and air that would make their double life his own. In their singleness of purpose each fought the other to get out into a world that seemed to them could never be vast enough to contain more than their own singularity. To be born first was to take everything. But even when the battle was won, the loser refused to give up. The will to live overcame even the will to singularity. The first child broke into the world with the hand of the second gripping tenaciously on to his heel – initially determined to hold the first back and pass him by, but when that failed, hanging on still, finally concluding that only the certainty of birth mattered. The first child won the race for the light, but the second had understood that survival might be a matter of manipulating chances, even if it meant admitting the existence of others and relinquishing the overwhelming certainty of self.

*

After their long internal battle and their birth, the infants Esau and Jacob lay side by side: oblivious strangers whose only similarity was that they breathed the same air. Rebekah's old nurse peered at them and shook her head.

'Two children,' she said.

'Twins,' gasped Rebekah, at last able to make sense of her torment.

'Two children,' the nurse repeated, continuing to shake her head.

It was true that they appeared quite unrelated. The first-born, Esau, was by far the larger of the pair, and seemed bigger still because he was so dark, his skin a deep olive and covered in a mantle of fine red hair, his head already capped with a thick russet mop. The face was crumpled and almost purple, eyes squeezed tight shut, but his mouth was a gaping black hole from which furious, staccato, nerve-searing cries emitted. Next to him, smooth-skinned and eerily calm, lay his brother Jacob. He did not cry. His eyes were wide and cloudless blue and seemed to peer beyond the examining faces into the far distance as if he were concentrating on something quite out of sight. While Esau screamed at the shock of an empty, uncircumscribed world and writhed and reached with flailing arms and legs to find its boundaries, Jacob lay still and watchful, as if taking his time to assess his new circumstances. There was no sign of the determined frantic ego that clung on to his older brother for dear life rather than risk being left behind in the dark. Birth had given Jacob pause for thought; for Esau it had set great confusion in motion.

In the moments after the birth, Rebekah was content to have regained possession of her own body and took no interest in what had emerged from it. But once the midwife had washed and swaddled the babies, she took them to their mother. Rebekah received a child in the curve of each arm, but under the still-screaming Esau her right arm remained stiff and unbending, while her left curled protectively around her silent, blue-eyed younger son. She looked into the faces of each in turn and then dropped her head back on the cushion, exhausted.

'One for him and one for me,' she whispered.

The boys grew, separate and disdainful of each other, further into what they already were from the moment of their birth, as what else can any of us do? Isaac watched his boys and saw two others in their demeanour. Esau, with his unruly red hair, always restless, dark-skinned, black eyes furtive under a heavy brow, muscular and strong, so physical, was increasingly uncontainable within the confines of the busy, orderly household, neatly encircled by herds of sheep and goats grazing peacefully in the outlying fields. Whereas everyone – even Isaac in his way – had a place in the community, Esau careened around the encampment, crashing into people and things, outside the control of his nurse or his mother, staring balefully at the munching herds in the fields when he wasn't actually charging at them or throwing stones to scatter the terrified beasts far and wide, to watch them race beyond the safe household boundaries towards the desert. He loved to see the herds disperse into the undefined, undomesticated space, and the herdsmen running like rats trying to gather them all back together again. Esau would not stay for his lessons or help with the work of the household. He exasperated everyone, either causing trouble or loafing darkly at the edge of the territory. Rebekah complained to Isaac.

'He's like a grain of sand in the eye. He won't listen to anyone, he refuses to keep still or do anything he's told. He won't learn. He won't work. He's like a wild animal. Greedy, noisy and rude. You've got to do something.'

'What?'

'Tell him he's got to behave.'

So Isaac told him.

'You've got to behave.'

The boy looked with black, blank eyes at his ailing, already virtually bedridden father, and once again, after so long, Isaac saw into the mysterious, dangerous and beautifully burning core of his brother Ishmael. There was the same pulsing energy, the raw life, the vivid challenge of physicality. The darkness and the gaze. Isaac cringed for a second before his son, and then tried to bring himself back to his position of authority.

'I am your father.'

The boy dropped his head down to one side.

'You must go to your lessons and learn things like your brother.'

'Why?'

'Because you are the oldest. You have to become a fit person to inherit and continue the line. So you must read and understand things about the world.'

'Why's J-J-Jacob fitter than me? He doesn't run f-f-fast, or climb trees. He spends all his time with Mo-Mo-Mo- Mother and her women.'

'He studies.'

'So do I.'

'You?'

'I s-ss-sss-study the wilderness. I go outside. I know what's around us. J-J-Jacob trips over stones. What's so f-f-fit about that? I'm stronger and faster and he just sits in corners looking d-d-d-down.'

Isaac remembered his pale, boyhood self. He remembered his glorious, furious brother striding into the wilderness to bring something of it back. Even with his stammer Esau reminded him of Ishmael.

'Well, then, perhaps you should go out with the hunters.'

The boy blinked an interest and waited, listening carefully now.

'You could learn to catch game. You'd be good at it, but you've got to learn about your prey. How to stalk and trap. And what to do with it once you've caught it. You like eating the game the hunters bring back, don't you?'

'Mmm, I love eating wild m-m-m-meat. Not all milky and t-t-tame like our slaughtered k-k-kids. Wild meat's d-d-d-different. It tastes of b-b-blood.'

'Yes, my boy. The taste in the mouth. Hunt for me, bring back game and make your father happy.'

'I want to hunt.'

'Yes.'

'I'll get you wild meat. I'll hide and then chase and run the beasts down and kill them and skin them and bring them back slung over my shoulder. And I'll cook them up good and strong and what a feast we'll have.'

The stammer all gone for a moment.

Isaac found his heart beating furiously at the thought that such a child as this, dark, hungry, energetic, alive, was his son. And Isaac loved Esau.

'Yes, you be a hunter, my son.'

So it came about that Isaac would not be a disgrace to the memory of Abraham; he was to have posterity and paternity, after all. The coming of fatherhood also confirmed Isaac's sonhood. For the first time since the searing moment on Mount Moriah, he considered himself something more than the boy whose father placed him on an altar and raised a cleaver above his head. He had become Isaac, son of Abraham, *father of Esau and Jacob*, instead of a dead end. There was to be a chain of succession, and he was a link in it; hope had not died with him. Indeed, there were two sons. A wealth of posterity. Isaac got up from his bed, and tried to trace his future in the receding shadow of the past. He could, perhaps, try for the adulthood that he had bypassed, going straight from youth to old age and infirmity, in his fearfulness of life. But there was still no word from the Lord. No voice whispered instruction into his waking ear, demanding his love and fidelity. No invisible force gave instructions to Isaac or made promises. It was true that the Lord had been silent since that day on Mount Moriah, even the great Abraham never heard from him again. But still, if Isaac was to continue the line of the chosen family, surely the God of Abraham ought to make it clear that he was also the God of Isaac? Isaac waited and listened, but heard nothing. His name was never called.

One morning Isaac sent word that the whole household was to come to his tent. Rebekah waited in the centre of the curious group. Isaac stood before them nervously, unused to making speeches, even to talking to more than one person at a time. His eyes darted about, finding and avoiding the barely patient gaze of his family and servants. Finally, his voice came in little breathy rushes.

'I've got something . . . to tell you all . . . We are going . . . There is a famine in the land . . . just as there was in my father's time.'

65

No one spoke though several eyebrows were raised in surprise. It was true that the crops had been poor that year and that the nearby pasture land was patchy. It would be necessary to make use of some of the stored feed that had been accumulated against such an emergency in past years, and the herds would have to be driven further for good grazing. But it was no one's idea of a famine, and certainly nothing like the great famine that had sent Abraham and his household to Egypt.

'Yes, there *is* a famine.' The voice became shrill at the bafflement he saw on his audiences faces. 'And the Lord has spoken . . . to me.'

In the shocked, expectant silence that attempted to absorb this news and waited for more, a single harsh laugh was heard.

'Ha! The Lord has spoken to you?' Rebekah repeated. 'He spoke to you? The god of Abraham spoke to you?'

'Yes. Yes, he did.'

'When?' she demanded, stepping forward and speaking to him as if they were quite alone and not in the midst of a public revelation.

'Last night. He spoke to me while I slept.'

'Oh, in a *dream*.'

'He spoke to me,' Isaac said resolutely, raising his voice now to make the message public again and retrieve it from Rebekah's scornful tone. 'The Lord said, *Do not go down into Egypt as your father did. Stay in the land that I will show you and I will be with you and bless you, because I swore an oath to Abraham your father. So I will multiply your seed like the stars in the heavens and give them all these lands, because Abraham listened to my voice and remained faithful to me.* So we will go west to Gerar and make a living from the land there.'

If the members of the household were astonished at Isaac's

sudden stirring after what had seemed a lifetime of passivity, they also recognised that a man can be changed and spurred on to achieve things when he becomes a father. And even if they thought it was an excessive response to a situation that was hardly extreme, most welcomed the move. The household of Isaac, son of Abraham, had been marking time for so long in that one place, living in the enervating centre of an energy vacuum that barely ticked over, that it seemed as if all progress was finished. People who have known great disruption fear change once stability is achieved, but their children, who have known nothing but stillness, long for a difference in the everyday of their lives. And even the old, after too long a quiet time, find their hearts beating faster at the prospect of something new. Good, there would be packing-up and preparation, travelling and relocation, the challenge of new geography, different people, new friends and enemies. Who or whatever was responsible for the sudden plan, they were glad of it. A plan of any kind, for any reason, was a sign of life and renewal. They left Isaac's tent celebrating.

Rebekah remained behind. She also felt a surge of excitement at something – anything – happening, but she remained wary as she questioned Isaac about his revelation.

'So you had a dream? What was he like, this Lord?'

'It was a vision,' Isaac spoke stubbornly. 'Visions come in dreams, you know, as well as in waking life. Some of Father's visions happened in dreams.'

'And some didn't. So what did this vision look like?'

'It wasn't that kind of a vision. I mean it was more of a voice, not a sight. I heard the voice of the God of Abraham . . .'

'The God of Abraham? Not the God of Isaac?'

She waited, but Isaac didn't answer.

'And he said he owed you a message because of your father?'

'I told you what he said.'

Rebekah shook her head.

'You can't even dream up a god of your own. Will you ever be your own man, even in your dreams? Will you ever be anything more than the shadow of your father?'

'It's just the way these things are said. *God of Abraham* includes me . . . It doesn't mean . . .' He heard the pleading in his voice and stopped himself. 'Don't argue with me. I'm not asking you a question, I'm telling you what is to happen. Now go and get ready, woman. The Lord has spoken to me. I am the head of this household. I am the patriarch.'

Rebekah swept out of the tent. But Isaac was disturbed. He certainly would have preferred it if the Lord had spoken to him in a waking vision. But the ways of the Lord . . . And it was true, though he hadn't noticed until Rebekah pointed it out, that the Lord had not used his name, only his father's, and that his words almost exactly echoed the phrases the Lord had spoken to Abraham. But he shook these thoughts away. He *was* the patriarch. He had sons and now he had received instructions.

Isaac took his household to Gerar in the west where after not too long a journey they pitched their tents and began to prepare for a new life. The locals took an interest in the arrival of the nomads from the east. They kept themselves to themselves, it was noted, but they paid for what they needed. New groups came and went. It kept life fresh and interesting. But Isaac worried about the interest the local men were showing. He had never lived among strangers before. And he remembered something his half-brother told him scornfully about his parents and how they had acquired their riches. He called Rebekah to him.

'Say that you're my sister. The way these men look at you.

You are a beautiful woman. What if they kill me to get their hands on you?'

Rebekah laughed and thought of her thick body, her aching legs, the disappointment that dragged down her features.

'More dreams?'

'My father had the same fear when he took Mother to Egypt. We are cautious men.'

'Very cautious. Are you going to repeat everything your father does? Will you be taking the children for a journey to Mount Moriah, too?'

Isaac gasped and began to shake. He opened his mouth to deny what she said, but only spasms of noise broke from him. Rebekah was alarmed. She was used to a man who retreated into passivity and blankness in the face of harshness, who protected himself from her barbs with deafness to her cruelty and blindness to her truths. Now he shuddered as if a terrible fever had taken hold of him. His words came suddenly in a torrent, a wall of noise.

'Don't say that. Don't talk like that. Don't ever mention that place . . . How dare you, how dare you speak . . . The Lord spoke to me, do you hear? Spoke to *me*. Don't ever talk about my father again. You know nothing, you came from nowhere. You are my wife. The Lord is with me. With *me*.'

'Then why must we pretend that you are my brother and not my husband? Won't this Lord of yours protect you?'

'Yes, but . . . yes, but we must . . . human action *complements* . . . yes, *complements* the wishes of the Lord. Human action . . . words fulfilled . . . Ah, ahh . . . my stomach . . . quick, put me to bed, my head hurts too . . .'

Rebekah was relieved that his symptoms took over from his fear and the dangerous thoughts that were not quite penetrating his mind. She called a servant and together they put him to bed.

Rebekah loved Jacob. There was nothing of Isaac about him that she could see. He was shorter and stockier than his wiry brother, but Jacob's fine smooth skin and long lashes above eyes of a blue that she thought she had never seen in nature only in dreams made him seem less bound to the earth than his brother. He was a quiet lad, but not a foolish one. He had his own ways, looking rather than doing, and a stillness which interspersed his physical movements so that he seemed never to be on his way to a destination, but idling with the world like a bird playing on an updraught. If he appeared languid, Rebekah knew that his mind was sharp. He learned the skills she had to show him and soaked up what his teachers told him. He knew when to pay attention. He knew why he had to learn. He stopped to look at things. He asked questions. He did not run when Esau laughed at him; he looked up from his studying and stared at his brother, quite expressionless, fathomless to Esau, who, getting no response he understood, gave a final hoot of derision and went off to slaughter some creature living its life and thinking itself free. Rebekah loved Jacob for that unperturbed stare at his scornful brother. She loved him for wanting the power of knowledge, for understanding the long game, at least that there might be one. Rebekah loved him for the future he had and for the difference he demonstrated between his father and his mother. Keep close, keep quiet, bide your time, she told him when he was a child. But she hadn't needed to. He had learned from that ancient struggle in the womb and for the light that only cunning could compete with dogged determination.

*

The old appetite in Isaac overcame his caution and his attempts to follow in even the most bizarre footsteps of his father. On market day, in the midst of Gerar and most of its population, Isaac whispered his desire in Rebekah's ear. He liked public displays of his physical ownership of her, and he could not resist it as they walked around assessing the livestock and pro- duce and comparing it to their own. When they sat in the shade of the public tea house discussing the purchase of breeding stock, Isaac's hand wandered towards Rebekah's thigh. He thought it surreptitious, or surreptitious enough. The hand slid under her haunch and probed for her privates under her robe. He was, after all, almost blind. To him, Rebekah had long since realised, his dimness was universal. He supposed others were blind to what he could not see. Rebekah had harsh words for him, but it was too late. Others had seen the Hebrew pawing at his sister and they talked to one another about it until word reached the ears of Abimelech, the ruler of the city. He sum- moned Isaac and charged him with scandalous behaviour.

'Is that how your people behave towards their families?' he demanded. 'You were seen playing sexually with your sister.'

'She's my wife,' Isaac explained, trembling. 'I called her my sister in case someone might desire her and kill me.'

Abimelech let out a harsh laugh.

'Your eyesight is worse than I thought. But what if thinking her unmarried one of my people had taken it into his head to take advantage of the poor woman?'

'My father, when he was in Egypt . . .'

'Yes, I've heard that story. The Pharaoh was no more impressed with your father's morals than I am with yours. Please keep your family to yourself. No one else wants them anyway.'

There was a good deal of laughter in Gerar about the strange fancies of the Hebrews. It was not hard for Isaac and his people to keep themselves to themselves.

To Rebekah's surprise the household of Isaac prospered. His herds multiplied and he grew rich and strong enough to make his neighbours envious. Rebekah watched in wonder as her hopeless and inadequate husband presided over their growing success. It was true that it was built on the wealth already accumulated by Abraham and passed on to Isaac. To that extent Rebekah was not surprised: if you have, you get more. She had learned that. But that Isaac was able to consolidate and increase his wealth, rather than merely keep it ticking along or losing the lot, gave her pause for thought until she realised that Isaac was still in his father's shadow. The absurdity of his pretence that she was his sister had been a nearly disastrous emulation of Abraham, but by keeping to Abraham's path, through repetition and mimicry, Isaac managed to do well in Gerar. Well enough in fact to get them exiled from the town. Abimelech ordered them to leave because their increasing wealth was threatening to the local population and therefore to his power. So the tents were pulled up and removed from the town to the adjacent valley outside Abimelech's authority.

Isaac had become more confident. He no longer spent most of his days in bed complaining of pains, but received his stewards' reports of how business was thriving. He seemed, very late in his life, to be growing into himself. His faint outline had strengthened until he was no longer pale and ghostlike but quite substantially in the world. Yet his new boundaries were drawn with Abraham's outline. Feeling himself growing into the mould of his father, Isaac began a tour of the wells that Abraham had dug many years before when he was marking out his territory. They had long been filled in by the local population, reasserting their prior, indeed actual territorial rights over the land, having been there in the first place. Now Isaac, his father's son, ordered a campaign of redigging Abraham's wells and renaming them as his father had named them. He began in the valley of Gerar but the local herdsmen claimed the well Isaac's men dug as their own. He tried again, and again a battle was threatened between Isaac's men and the local people. So he moved further away. This time no one disputed the well. It was wilderness. And so the land became the land of the son of Abraham. He took his household up to Beersheba, where his father had dug a well and built an altar to his Lord. And that night, according to Isaac, the Lord came again to him in a dream.

'Another dream?' Rebekah said.

'Yes. A vision. He came to me, as he came to my father.'

Rebekah looked sceptical but did not say anything.

'He said, in my vision, "I am the God of Abraham, your father. Do not fear, for I am with you and will bless you and will multiply your seed for the sake of my servant Abraham."'

Rebekah shook her head at her poor substitute of a husband. 'So?'

'So I am going to build an altar and dig a well. And I shall call the place Beersheeba.'

'There is already an altar and a well. It is already called Beersheba. Your father has done that.'

'But now I will do it.'

But even as he spoke Rebekah saw the energy begin to seep out of Isaac. Even he was not entirely deaf to the meaning behind his words. She saw him wince as if an old pain had reasserted itself. And she could not help but feel relieved. She

73

was too old for life suddenly to take a turn for the better. It would only remind her how much time, how much of her youth and adulthood had been spent in misery. Better now could only be worse.

So things reverted safely to what they had been. Isaac having made his bid for independence and seen it to be no more than an empty echo of his father, returned to his bed and his physical suffering. He was always at death's door, just like in the old days. And then, to consolidate Rebekah's self-righteous misery, Esau married, not one but two women from the local area, Judith and Bashemath, Hittites. Esau, most comfortable outside the boundaries of the family, had now married outside its boundaries too. There was a good deal of screaming and shouting from Rebekah at Esau and at Isaac. Esau was baffled, and Isaac was mortified, made even more unwell at this weakening of the line of Abraham, but it was done. The thuggish son had gone out and found himself some common local women. *Isaac's* son, she told her husband, again and again. Isaac, who had not even been trusted by his father to choose his own bride, now had not managed to prevent his favourite son from marrying out, scorning the line, disregarding the covenant between Abraham and his Lord that the seed of Abraham, not its dilution, would inherit the earth. Caring nothing for past or future, Esau had married his luscious local girls and both Rebekah and Isaac, each for their own reasons, were dismayed.

The sharp scent of the spiced meaty stew reached Isaac before the sound of his son's footsteps across the threshold of the tent. Isaac's mouth watered at the pleasure he was about to experience.

'F-Father?'

The voice was gruff, but nervous. There was uncertainty in

the salutation. But who was blind and who could see? Who else if not 'father'?

'Here I am. Who are you, my son?'

A foolish question, a joking response to the query in his son's voice, but something made him want a reply, nevertheless. Not *something*. It was the wrong voice.

'I am Esau, your heir. I've d-d-one what you asked. Sit up, please, and eat my game so that you can give me your solemn b-blessing.'

'But how could you have caught and cooked it so quickly, my son?'

'Because the lord your G-G-God made it easy for me.'

Isaac's stomach craved the stew whose smell and warmth now filled the tent. Even so, Isaac's other senses were not quite dead.

'Come here, please, so that I can touch you, my boy, to see whether or not you are my son Esau.'

His son squatted beside the bed without a murmur. The right son would have protested at the absurdity of his father's distrust. Isaac reached out and received a pair of hands in his own. They were rough-skinned, working hands covered with hair. He hadn't realised Esau's hands were quite so coarse, so animal. It was a long time since he had been able to see him clearly, but . . . He shook his head.

'The voice is Jacob's but the hands are Esau's.'

He waited, but there was silence.

'Are you my son, Esau?'

A rare and dangerously direct question from Isaac.

'I am,' his son replied.

What blame could fall on Isaac? He had asked a question and received an answer.

'Well then, serve me so that I can eat what my son has caught and give him my solemn blessing.'

Isaac ate with relish, and it seemed to him that he had no choice. Perhaps it was the irresistible smell and taste of the food, which was exceptionally delicious and lived up fully to its aroma, or perhaps it was that there was something about the way his son had used the word 'heir'. Isaac loved Esau, and of course wanted his oldest and most beloved son to inherit. But something at the back of his mind made him not want to doubt that this, whoever it was, was indeed his heir. Even so, even chewing away happily, he hesitated once again.

'Come closer, my son, and kiss me.'

Isaac used his senses one last time, as he embraced the young man and sniffed carefully at his neck. It was Esau's smell that came from his son's robe. Unmistakable. The smell of sweat and earthy, physical work. The smell of the world. Jacob smelt of musty interiors, of ink and scrolls. It would do. How much proof must an old man have in order to do what had to be done? No one could say he hadn't been cautious. He was a blind old man, on his deathbed. What more could be expected of him?

Isaac put down his bowl and, placing his hands on his heir's head, blessed his son.

'God grant you the best the earth has to offer. Let people serve you and nations bow down to you. You will be your brother's master. May God curse those who curse you and those who bless you be blessed.'

It was done and Isaac's heir left hastily, in silence. Isaac did not mind, he settled back to enjoy his stew.

He had barely got a spoonful into his mouth when he heard a familiar voice calling as it neared the tent.

'Rouse yourself, Father, here comes your son with the stew from the game he caught so you can eat it and give me the solemn blessing.'

How could he ever mistake that rough, common voice?

'Who are you?' Isaac said as the footsteps entered his tent. Not that he didn't know, only that he was playing for time.

'I'm your s-s-son,' Esau babbled, perplexed. 'Your heir, your f-f-firstborn, Esau.'

Isaac dropped the spoon, his hand trembling so violently that he was unable to hold it. The truth was too close, too known, to be acknowledged.

'Who was it, then, who caught the game and brought it to me before you came. Look. And received my blessing? Who's blessed can't be unblessed.'

Esau didn't have to wonder. He fell to his knees and wailed his panic and loss. 'B-b-bl-less me too, Fa-fa-father.'

'Your brother deceived me and he's taken your blessing.'

Not his fault. A blind, sick, deceived old man. No, not his fault at all. Hadn't he intended to bless Esau, his favourite, his oldest son? Even if he wasn't . . . He had wanted to bless his beloved Esau.

'Jac-Jac-Jac-Jacob. He tried to pull me back at bi-bir-birth, then he t-t-took my b-birthright and now look, he's stolen my b-b-b-blessing. Haven't you saved anything to b-less me with?'

Obviously, it was terrible, but there was nothing to be done, Isaac thought. Jacob had been given everything. He had been deceitful enough, clever enough, to take it. Isaac had a small moment of admiration for his trickster son, though all his love was for his simple child.

'I made him your master and promised him the grain and wine – all of it. He inherits everything. What can I do, my son?'

Esau dropped his head on to his father's bed, the smell of two gamey stews stinking in his nostrils. He pawed at his father's robe as if physical closeness might change matters.

'Nothing? Have you nothing to give me, my fa-fa-father?' and suddenly he was weeping. Hiccupping sobs like a small boy in pain. 'Fa-fa-father. Bl-bl-bless me too, Fa-father.' He lay his head against Isaac's faint heart and the tears soaked through the cloth and dampened his father's chest. An old, tired, guilty hand stroked his betrayed, beloved son.

'You will live from what the earth can provide. You will live by your sword, a warrior, a hunter, and you will be your brother's underling. But one day, you will rebel, and be free. That is all I can offer you, my son.'

But already Esau had pulled away from his father's embrace and left the tent. There was nothing more that Isaac could do. He reached down to the ground and found one of the bowls of stew that his sons had left. They certainly weren't piping hot any more, but there was no point in wasting them.

It was Rebekah's old nurse who, passing by Esau's tent and hearing a grown man sniffing and weeping, stopped and over-heard his mutterings to himself.

'Jacob, Jacob, Jacob . . . My brother. As soon as my father's dead and buried I'll settle with Jacob, my brother. I'll kill him. That Jacob . . .'

The grimly fluent words trailed away into sobs of fury and deprivation.

Rebekah received the news of Esau's reaction with surprise. Her plan had been made on the spur of the moment. She had considered only its success, not its aftermath. Had she believed that fraternity would take care of Esau's resentment at the theft of his primogeniture? Of course the plan had worked. In his head, if not his heart, Isaac knew as well as she that Jacob was by far the better son to inherit the line. All she had done was provide him with an excuse to do what he knew needed doing, in spite of his terror of contravening convention. How could he possibly have believed, really believed, in the charade that Rebekah had arranged? If he loved Esau so much, could goat's skin and mere greed have fooled him? She had taken any curse on herself, but Isaac had not cursed Jacob when he found out the truth, he had merely confirmed it for Esau. No, yet again, she had done the family a service.

But she had not thought about how Esau might feel. Nor how he might react. And now she was frightened. She could manage situations, push them this way and that in order to get what she wanted, but she could not control an unloved son's violent rage. She was scared of her oldest son. She suspected that his capacity to hunt and kill animals could as easily be transferred to a human prey if he was pushed far enough. He had no learning, only responses. And now he wept and comforted himself with promises of his brother's death.

She called Jacob to her.

'Esau is dangerous. He is consoling himself with thoughts of killing you as soon as your father dies. He hates you and he could act on it. You must go away. Go and stay with my brother, Laban, in Haran. Wait and let Esau's anger subside. He'll probably forget about it when he's spent some time hunting and whoring with his wives. I'll keep an eye on things, and when it's safe, I'll send for you.'

Jacob hardly protested. He had been lingering nervously in his tent, keeping well away from his howling, wrathful brother. He did not plan to confront him. But for Rebekah it was a final blow. At his birth she lost her older son, unable to love him, and all that remained of love in her life, Jacob, her true son, her hope, was now to be lost to her as well. As Jacob prepared to flee from his home, Rebekah sat in her tent and wept. Now she had nothing left but time. Still, she pulled herself together for one last effort.

She entered Isaac's tent and saw him sleeping soundly. He snorted at her entrance as if something dark had entered his dreams.

'Isaac, wake up.'

He jerked awake. Rebekah paced up and down beside his bed. He heard her voice, stretched like a skin to breaking point, as it passed from one end of him to the other.

'I hate my life, do you hear, I hate it. How can I ever hold my head up in public when our son brings these Hittite women into our household? Dreadful creatures. The shame of it. How could you just have let it pass like that? I'll tell you something, if Jacob takes a wife from the native women, my life won't be worth anything. Not to me. I'm telling you, if such a thing happened to me, I don't know what I'd do, but it would be final.'

Isaac sighed. Esau had married his wives some time ago. Why was Rebekah suddenly so upset? But who knew when Rebekah was going to be upset? Ach, hadn't he had enough distress lately? His beloved son no longer spoke to him, and refused to go out hunting. No love, no good food. He had lost everything, and just because he had been tricked. An old, tired, dying man. It was enough to make you weep. Who had ever loved him? Where was the respect a man of his age and his condition deserved?

But anything for a bit of peace and quiet. If Rebekah was going to fuss about Hittite women, nothing would stop her unless she got what she wanted.

'What do you want me to do about it?' Isaac said faintly, knowing that there must be something.

'Send him away. Send Jacob away from his brother's bad influence.'

Isaac was as businesslike as it was possible for him to be when Jacob arrived to hear what his father had to say.

'Your mother's worried about you marrying out, like Esau. It would be best for everyone if you went to stay with your uncle Laban and found a wife from his family. I did. Look how well it has turned out.'

Jacob looked carefully at his father to see if there was anything approaching grim humour on his face. There wasn't.

'You have my blessing. You've had my blessing. You are my legitimate heir whether anyone likes it or not. So: I hope the God of Abraham blesses you and all your offspring. There you are.'

It was a formal farewell, not the blessing of a loving father to a beloved son. Jacob would have to be content with the tears of his mother watering his cheek as he bid her goodbye.

A few days later Esau entered his father's tent for the first time since he lost the blessing.

'F-f-father?'

Isaac sniffed the air. It carried no scent of game.

'F-f-father, I overheard what you said to Jacob before he left, about marrying out. I didn't understand. I didn't know you cared so much about my Hittite wives. I can see now . . . I've dis-dis-disappointed you. But, look, I've made up for it. I went to see my uncle Ishmael, your half-brother, and he's given me his daughter, Mahalath, as a wife. So I'm going to be married to a rel-rel-rel-relative, just like you want.'

Isaac waved his son away wearily. His beloved son had married his beloved brother's daughter in order to regain the love of his father. As if that would make everything all right. As if it wasn't too late, far, far too late for anything to be all right. Isaac turned over on his side and noted the weakness of his heartbeat, the shallowness of his breath. He was hungry, too.

2

And so on. And so forth. Round and round and on and on. How early in the telling of the story of family the pattern emerges. One generation, two, and already the serpent is chasing its tail. Family, not-family, love, not-love, duty and consequences. But no surprises, even so soon, no surprises. Not that *they* would have thought that, living in the now of the story as they had to. All surprise to them. Nothing worse had happened or would happen to anyone in the world than had happened to Rebekah, and to Isaac, because of course, it had happened to them. Tell them a story with uncanny similarities to their own about X, Y and Z and they would think: no surprises, an old story. Perspective is everything. Whatever is you is new. You are not part of a plot, you are living your life. Tell that to an editor.

Perhaps niggling in his dreams, or in the deep, unwordy recesses of his mind, Jacob might have noted the repetition – already – of another's story in his own. But which human wants to confront the possibility that they are in a different narrative from the one they thought they were in? And by the time the editor has taken up the various stories and redacted them into an overall coherence (yes, yes, the editor's coherence, but coherence nevertheless) whose story belongs any longer to its narrator? Be an editor, I say, not a story-teller. Have the last word. That much I've learned.

So when, many decades ahead, Jacob, now in his near dotage, stared down at the torn and bloody rag that had been placed in his hand, he had no thought of fathers before and after that moment also confronting the loss of a beloved son.

'Do you recognize this? Is it your son's tunic or not?' they asked the old man.

His hand shook and his eyes dimmed, but he hardly looked at or felt the material before he echoed confirmation. Barely drew breath, let alone thought, before he blurted out, choking on a sob:

'I recognize it. It is my son's tunic. A wild animal has torn my Joseph, beloved Joseph, firstborn of Rachel, to pieces.'

Then the sob became a howl and his tragedy shuddered through him. He tore his clothes, his already watery blue, receding old eyes flooded with tears, and he plunged into deep mourning, day after day, from dawn until dark, shouting, weeping and wailing his incomparable bereavement as if mourning had become his profession. He could not be consoled. His sons, his other sons, tried to calm him; his remaining wife, his concubines, they gathered round the distraught old man, but nothing alleviated his pain; the loss of his favourite, his joy, his clever, beautiful boy was not to be assuaged. What comfort could there be for the everything that he had lost? For all the love in his life drained and gone or never been? For his always-present barely suppressed terror that there was no God, no meaning, for him, as there had been for his monumental grandfather, Abraham, and even for his tremulous father, Isaac? Mourning for the denial, the despoiling of the whole point of his whole existence?

'Comfort? You offer me comfort? I will go to my grave still mourning.'

He is inconsolable, his family told one another in varying tones, but all gradually shading towards resentment. Jacob neither knew nor cared what they thought. His loss was monumental. His life was to be rounded with mortal sadness. After those things. After all that. After everything, everything turned out to have been nothing. Love had betrayed him all his life.

As a boy, sitting in tents learning and building pictures of the future, Jacob had dreamed a life for himself. He felt his life beginning, sensed the start of a shape, a trajectory, and followed it in his imagination as it made a smooth upward arc, a fluid leap towards a plateau of manhood and substance, and then a graceful dip towards calm, completion, serenity: the quiet illumination of a long life well lived. His vision. A youthful arrogance, he now saw, a certainty of pattern that reminded him of his favourite son, so clever, so knowing, so unaware of the complexity and feelings of those who were not him. He loved Joseph all the more for his wide-eyed clever pronouncements that took no account of the world and the feelings of others. Jacob saw himself in Joseph, before the purity of living in tents disappeared.

Jacob too had been a beloved child. Beloved of his mother, as Joseph could not be. He had basked in Rebekah's love of him and her preference for him over his older, coarser twin brother. He lived in the light of her eyes, warmed by her glow of pride at his recitations and knowings. Therefore, he could live without the love of his father. So he told himself. Who would need the love of a father who doted on his brother Esau in preference to him? What would such a love be worth? So Rebekah told him, so he understood. A foolish old man, bedridden, blind and tormented with mysterious ailments, dying daily, but always alive the following morning. A fuss of an old man. Who wanted such love? Except it seems that a child wants a father's love, wants a father to see his qualities of heart and mind, and Jacob wondered in spite of himself why his father warmed only to his brother, dark and vile as he was, with his tangled chaotic curls, all physical. Why he doted on the hunter, the man of the wilderness who knew nothing, who lived entirely in the present, with no imagination for the meaning of his heritage or inheritance – for the weight of what had been achieved and how to shoulder the precious burden. A grubby oafish man who flinched from thought, guileful only against deer and rabbit. *And Isaac loved him.* Or loved the result of what he did. Loved the sharp smell of blood and fear on his hands and the taste of wild meat in his mouth. The son who thought and read and pondered about the nature of a life, about the shape and trajectory of a full existence, he cared for not at all. Each, in his way, was his ghostly, timorous father's son. But blank physicality and unthinkingness was what his father loved: action and stupidity. To Jacob, it was incomprehensible. Still, he *was* beloved, and by the parent with the strongest character, with the better judgement, who knew what a life might be, who sensed that it was Jacob who would carry the family name into the future. So Jacob had the mother, and Esau the father, and each life was set.

Jacob sat in tents and learned. Esau roamed the wilderness and hunted.

How strange then that the smooth, pale, thoughtful son who sat in tents bent over his scrolls should be the one to find himself sent into exile – should be the one, indeed, who caused himself to be sent into exile, in fear of his life. And the other, who had seemed uncontainable, the wanderer, the wilderness child – he remained within the bounds of family, weeping for the loss of familial blessing he had brought on himself by selling his birthright, distraught at having his inheritance stolen from under his nose. The wily hunter was not the wily man. Jacob was the wily man, an actor, a deceiver, it turned out; so much trickier than he had imagined himself to be. His desire for posterity had overcome any reticence about turning tradition upside down, and lying came as easily in his own cause as if it were truth itself. He startled himself, but he hoped he might return to his tent and his sedentary learning, his desires having been gratified. For all his learning Jacob was surprised to discover that after all it was he who was expelled from his home and family. Clever, perhaps, devious certainly, but not wise. It seemed that sitting in tents was not quite enough.

The old man that Jacob became, who had lost his favourite wife and now his favourite son, remembered that time when, long ago, he had mislaid his place in the world in spite of, because of, his efforts to secure it. The quiet studious boy who sat in tents had taken a risk, had put on the mask of his brother, dark, hairy, smelling of blood, and offered his father both sons simultaneously. Only in the guise of Esau could Jacob gain his father's love and promise of future. He had not thought that the risk he took when he put on his brother's clothes was that he might *become* his brother, a wanderer, a hunter of sorts, all the

87

simplicity of sitting and studying lost in the complexity of looking for somewhere and someone to be. Loss and gain in equally
terrifying measure. A life doubled and stripped simultaneously
by a duplicitous act. Action overcame knowledge and Jacob's
new world for evermore would lack the easy coherence of
studying in tents. That fine trajectory he had envisioned as a
boy had lost its graceful arc and become an unknown line, as all
lives are unknown lines once one becomes old enough to realise
it. Unknown and, of course, known – depending always on
whose story is being told by whom, and who, of course, is revis-
ing it. But as Jacob took leave of his mother, her hands pressed
down in blessing on his head, her tears falling on to his knees,
Jacob felt his pattern tremble and break. The darkness inside his
shut lids was the same darkness that the future held.

He walked into an empty space of a life that was no longer
safely bounded. He left his home, all he had ever known, and
with none of the comforts or familiarities of his former existence he entered into the wilderness, the terrain of his brother,
heading north to become a stranger, away from his twin whose
rage was more dangerous even than the blank unknown of the
desert, and away from the father who lay trembling abed, afraid
of his own shadow.

Jacob left Beersheba and set out for distant Haran. It was the
first time that he had walked alone in one direction without the
intention of returning to the place he had set out from the same
day. It was the first time that night fell in a place where he was
completely alone and empty-handed. And it fell so suddenly.
Like an immense wall, miraculously and instantaneously
dropped in front of him and behind him. He was not used to
the pitch-black of the desert night, he had never known darkness that came with such sudden ferocity. Deadly darkness

belonged to the outskirts of the household, marking the bound-aries of security. It was to be observed from a distance. Even from a distance it made you shudder. The servants lit lamps around the compound and in the tents long before the sun dis-appeared below the horizon. And you took comfort from the distant darkness that you were in the light. Now he was immersed in unilluminated night. He stopped dead. He was solitary and unsustained as he had never before been in his life. He trembled at what might be beyond the circle of surrounding blackness – at the thought of his brother catching up with him and breaking through the night to take his revenge. But much as he feared the violence of Esau, he also profoundly wished to absent himself from his own terror. He was consumed with a desire to become small against the vastness of empty night and to feel the solid ground beneath him. A great weariness came over him. He felt around the desert floor in the blackness and found a sizeable rock which he placed beside his head as he lay down. Perhaps he kept it close by so that he might have some-thing to defend himself with should his brother attack him in the darkness. Or was it there by his head as a gift, a handy weapon for Esau to use to exact his punishment, who in his haste and rage and thoughtlessness might have left home empty-handed? Jacob did not think either of those things, wished for neither death nor life. He merely put his head down beside the stone and fell instantly into a deep sleep.

He dreamed some kind of consolation. In a stream of light created by neither moon or stars, a host of beings peopled his loneliness: in oneiric slow motion the creatures, somewhat human in form, climbed and descended a ramp that sloped gently but persistently upward beyond the range of sight. Their various comings and goings up and down seemed purposeful, as an ant turning abruptly in its path and proceeding in quite another direction appears purposeful to an observer who could not imagine such a sudden rerouting to be entirely meaningless. The beings showed no concern with the small form that lay curled tight and still in the pool of their light at the foot of the ramp. If they had eyes they did not look at him. Nonetheless, Jacob was bathed in life and light as he had not been when he went to sleep. In his dream, a voice, or a sort of voice, spoke: 'I am the Lord, the God of Abraham your father and the God of Isaac.' It went on to promise him all that had been promised to Abraham, the land, the heritage, and more, a great bursting forth of life and future. It offered him solace for the fact of being alone. 'Look, I am with you, I will keep you safe wherever you go and I will bring you back to your own place. I will not leave you until it is over.'

Now he had the promise. A dreamed promise, it was true, not the face-to-face covenant that the Lord and Abraham had made, but a voice and a promise nevertheless that placed him in the direct line. And in something more than the direct line. His dream voice had given him Abraham as a father, not Isaac. And he felt great relief in his dream: recognised as the right son of the right father. Given his due. Let Esau have Isaac. Abraham, the uncle of his mother, was his true father. He, Jacob, was next in line for the promise of Abraham's Lord. It was, in his dream, as it should be, as it always should have been. Isaac faded forever into anomaly and Jacob slept dreamlessly on until it was time to wake and continue the future that his grandfather had started.

He woke in the morning full of his dream and felt stronger. He had a promise and a purpose. Even so, promise or no promise, bearer of posterity or not, Jacob knew, if anyone did, that treachery lurked in even the closest relationship.

'In this place, I have heard the voice of the Lord of Abraham,' he said solemnly, for all that he was quite alone, allowing the words to be blown by the desert wind in the direction perhaps of the ears of the Lord. 'I will call this place Bethel, and I will set this stone that lay beside me in the night as an altar to him and make this a holy place . . . *if*, as he said, the Lord is with me and guards me and keeps me fed and clothed and protected and remains with me until I return safely to my father's house. If it all comes out as promised, then the Lord of Abraham will be my Lord and I will build an altar to him in Bethel.'

He had reiterated the deal, adding a few specific details to the generality spoken by the Lord in the dream and offering something of his own into the bargain, conditional of course on things going well. He waited for a word or a sign of agreement, a reassurance that the Lord would indeed be with him, that the deal was ratified, but there was nothing, not even the sound of the wind, which had dropped suddenly. Jacob wondered if he could feel the protection of the Lord but couldn't identify any new sense of safety. Still, he didn't know if it was a thing that was experienced all the time, or just something that happened when it was necessary. He looked at the stone which had lain beside him all night and reissued his ultimatum.

'Here I will raise this stone and make an altar to the Lord, if everything turns out all right,' he repeated sonorously. Again there was nothing but desert around him, no inkling of the love of the Lord, no frisson of security. The words hung in the hot dusty air, seeming to inhabit the place. So Jacob left the stone where it lay and set off, alone it seemed to him, and in fact, with nothing but his staff, northwards and east towards Haran.

*

Being alone was nothing new for Leah. Her best moments had come to her in childhood, when she was on her own. In quiet spots away from the regular paths and in empty corners of rooms she conjured up the possibilities of her life, the finest times, the happiest days and nights of all her days to come. She had dreamed up whisperings she could hardly understand, spoken gently into her ear where others only heard the sound of the wind in the branches of the pomegranate trees or the water trickling deep in the underground spring or the distant shout of her mother looking for her to get on with her chores. If the whisperings contained no actual words that she could decipher, they were entirely clear to her childish imaginings. They cherished and wove the finest strands of gossamer around her; they enclosed her as if she were a jewel so precious that its light was to be observed only by a single viewer, the only one who could see it without being blinded by its power. The whispering uncovered her, revealing her dazzling facets for herself and the whisperer alone. But although the whispering was only to be heard in the silence when she was separated from others, it promised her relief from solitude, and an understanding that made her weep with joy.

'Beautiful,' the whisper went. 'You are so beautiful, Leah, my Leah.'

That was all it ever said; all it ever needed to say. With those words it said everything and painted a picture of all the happiness of her life.

The silence in which the whisperings could thrive was always broken, of course, in the regular business of family life. But she only needed a moment or so each day to build the world of her future.

The present, in between the whisperings, offered a different prospect.

'It would have been better if she had been a boy,' she had heard the women say when as a child she lay among them pretending to sleep. Gradually, she understood that they meant her. More gradually she understood why. She began to learn about the present by watching her little sister run to and fro between the women while she lay with her eyes so nearly shut that she saw only flickering images through a shimmering curtain of eyelash. Rachel ran laughing between her mother and aunts and the servants who held their arms out to catch her in her game of landing on the soft giving and willing flesh of one after another. Then they would say in an undertone over the head of Rachel and intended to be beyond the sleeping ears of Leah how it would have been better had Leah been born a boy. *Because she was not pretty. Because she could not charm the world with her laugh and her enticing smile. Because she was not Rachel.*

'Well, not ugly. She isn't ugly, but plain, let's say.' They tried to find just the right definition for her deficiencies. 'It isn't that Rachel is beautiful . . . no, she *is* lovely, in fact beautiful, but it's not that Leah isn't beautiful . . . lots of girls aren't beautiful . . . but she isn't . . . *striking*.' They would test all manner of descriptions to explain what it was about Leah that made it a pity she wasn't a boy, but it was hard to put a finger on it. In the end they fell back always on the contrast with her little sister, who was indeed beautiful, *but apart from that*, had something about her, a charm, a light in her eyes, a curve of the mouth, that made one want to reach out, to capture and enclose her delightful running body into one's arms. Leah never ran towards anyone knowing that she would land safe and sound, encircled by them. It could not have happened. Neither the running towards nor the encirclement. Finally, the conversation about what, exactly, it was about Leah that made her utterly not Rachel, was finalised.

'The eyes. Something weak about the eyes. Too pale, too small, the lashes too short, the line of the lid too indistinct . . . oh, something anyway about the eyes.'

It seemed to satisfy. The women never mentioned Leah again while she pretended to sleep and soon she was too old to nap, and instead remained awake with them, mending and preparing food beside them, learning their women's skills. They were perfectly kind to her, leaning forward and showing her how to do this stitch properly, how to grind the wheat to such a consistency. She was just like one of them. Rachel, when she grew too old for the naps she naughtily refused to have, spent little time sequestered with the women but raced, ignoring their half-hearted cries of 'come back', and spent the long afternoons running with the village boys or sitting with the shepherds and goatherds laughing and basking in their admiration. Whatever it was about her meant that she did not have to apply herself to learning what women had to know, did not have to do anything that her spirit rebelled against. Leah did not hate Rachel, but she knew the nature and degree of their difference. And long after the women had stopped wondering about what was wrong with her, Leah spent solitary moments gazing into reflecting surfaces at her eyes. It was true, she could see what they had meant. Something about the eyes. Something not enough. Something absent. Not Rachel.

The whispered voice that told her she was beautiful disappeared as time went on. She continued to seek out solitary places in the hope of hearing it, but there was only silence. Still, there was the memory of the whispering and of the expectation of happiness, of finding her place in the world. The memory stayed strong. She continued also to look at her eyes whenever the opportunity arose. Sometimes – increasingly – she wept as she looked, mourning the loss of what she had not yet had but which she remembered expecting, and she looked as she wept, noting the smallness of her eyes as they stared out at her, and the raw redness around the lids. She watched the watery colour of her pupils become all the more vapid, a blue so pale that it tended towards colourlessness when washed with tears. The women were right, it was her eyes. And she cried extra tears for the absurdity of her misfortune. Rachel had large, blazing eyes, stark violet blue, heavily lashed. Her younger sister had the luck to have good, strong eyes. And as if they concurred with her sadness, Leah's eyes weakened over the years, until, by the time she was fifteen, they saw little that wasn't directly in front of her. She had to screw them up and peer at anything that was more than an arm's length distant, making them yet paler and more watery with strain, and even smaller. She believed it was weeping that had caused her eyes to deteriorate. Rachel's eyes were those of a wheeling bird, she saw clearly to any horizon; but then when had Rachel ever cried, other than momentarily when some desire or other was briefly frustrated? Certainly, Leah was sure that Rachel had never cried alone.

When Jacob arrived, Leah recognised his voice immediately. Though he said nothing more than a polite 'hello' and that he was pleased to meet his other cousin, and his eyes could barely drag themselves away from the vision of Rachel for long enough to glance at her, Leah heard her past and the future it had spoken of in his voice, which was – there was no doubt about it – that of her old whisperer.

Beautiful, you are so beautiful, Leah, my Leah.

She had never forgotten, and now, with the coming of Jacob,

she realised that she had been always waiting for the owner of the voice to arrive. She forgave the intervening silence and all her tears. The one who whispered her future had at last entered her life.

But Rachel was flushed and her eyes brilliant when she arrived back with their new-found cousin. All evening she fidgeted, unable to keep still or remain in one place, and her breath came fast and light. She laughed a lot, a high bright sound, even in the silences, though she said nothing, not a word. Their father, Laban, looked hard at the face and manner of his youngest daughter, and welcomed Jacob to his house.

The solitude was as much a hardship as the baking heat of day, the freezing cold of night, the jagged rocks and endless dust of the desert trek. Jacob thought he knew solitude in his tents of learning, but a tent is a contained place. The desert loneliness extended in all directions, even to his heart that ached with bleakness. There were places where nomads met, wells where they watered their beasts and exchanged information, but he was a stranger among them. Who travelled the desert alone with nothing but poor clothes and a staff? Whether they thought him mad or in flight from some crime, they looked on him with suspicion, and although they did not refuse him water and rest, they did not offer any other kind of human hospitality. They were right, Jacob concluded. He was in flight, travelling alone, with nothing, escaping, exiled; he was marked even to himself as an outcast. He walked doggedly on, never thinking of his destination, only of his point of departure and what was lost. Of all the deprivations, the solitude was the worst. It was like death, without hope of succour, a leaving behind of everything familiar, a heading towards a blank personless unknown. The dream promises of the Lord were of little help. Where was the warmth, the comfort he had been offered? Where was the voice, the 'I am with you'? If the voice had been real, it had now deserted him. Not even in birth had he been so alone. A twin wrenched apart from his brother, his family, his home. Alone in the world, and, everything in his body and mind knew, it was not how it was supposed to be. This was the terrible punishment for his crime against family, his assault on love. It was too harsh a retribution for what, after all, had been in the best interests of the family. Alone, Jacob was easily persuaded that he was unjustly punished. The whole family were implicated in the conspiracy to deprive Esau of his birthright, but only he suffered exile and alienation. The desert made him weep for himself, but he was strong and young and had all the physical will to survive its hardships. Jacob wept with fury from time to time, but he kept walking to Haran.

Many weeks later, he came to a well where a group of shepherds were gathered with their flocks. Haran, he knew, was not far off.

'Where are you from?' he asked them.

'Haran,' they said, assessing and then dismissing the stranger as a wanderer of no consequence, a foreigner. They turned their backs and continued their talk.

'Do you know Laban, son of Nahor?' Jacob insisted.

One of them turned casually.

'We know him.'

'Is he well?'

His questions had the abruptness of one who had wandered for too long alone. But now the shepherds, hearing Laban's name spoken with familiarity, reckoned him a little more carefully. He was dishevelled and tattered from his long journey, but he spoke like an educated man; perhaps he had business with Laban. They gave up their conversation and concentrated on the short but strong-looking traveller.

'He's well.'

'It's still daylight and plenty of grazing time left, why not get on with watering the sheep instead of standing around chattering?'

The shepherds looked at one another in astonishment. Only someone with a right to say such things would dare to say them to a group of able-bodied young men who could overwhelm a weary stranger with ease. The tramp had to be more than he seemed. It would be best to wait and see before they laid into him for his impertinence.

'We wait until all the flocks are gathered and the stone is rolled away from the well,' the oldest said in a toneless voice, waving one of his group back with a pacifying wave of his arm. 'Look, there's Laban's daughter Rachel arriving to water her father's sheep.'

There was a massive stone covering the mouth of the well. When all the local flocks had arrived, several of the strongest shepherds would roll it away and the sheep were watered. Rachel shepherded her father's flock towards the well with a bright smile, anticipating her regular meeting with the lads she had grown up and roamed wild with. They came morning and evening to chatter and laugh and talk together, as young people do, while the sheep drank their fill. Jacob watched her light-footed approach, saw the energy, her youth, the play in her movements, the sway of her hips, the tilt of her head, the smile of anticipated pleasure on her mouth, a gleam of life in her eyes, and his heart ached to breaking point with all the dusty, solitary, desert days he had passed.

As Rachel approached, he ran to the great stone at the mouth of the well, and with all the loss and loneliness of his recent life balled tightly into energy, he embraced the stone in his arms, barely able to encompass the half of it, and heaved with all his might. There was always physical strength in him, unused in his days of learning, but now there was more, not just from the hardening brought about by his wilderness trek, but from the flowering of a massive will to unblock the opening to the well, to welcome the bright, warm creature who approached, to begin to make reparation to the ordinary world that he had violated. He wanted also to be noticed by her. Rachel, they said.

The stone inched away from its lodgement under the pressure of Jacob straining and pulling at it and intensifying his effort until there was no longer any danger of it rolling back into place, then he changed his posture and braced his whole being against one side of it and pushed, himself and it, out of the way of the mouth of the well. The great stone rolled unwillingly a short distance, but far enough, and Jacob lay, draped over it for a moment, recovering some of his breath. The shepherd lads looked at one another making grimaces and shaking limp hands up and down, impressed by the feat, and then smirked, acknowledging the motive for the feat as Rachel arrived and gazed wonderingly at the rock, and Jacob, solitary, breathing hard beside it. Usually she liked to watch four or five of the boys manhandling the stone out of the way and join in their whoops of satisfied combined effort as the opening to the well was revealed.

Rachel stood shyly, with her eyes to the ground, as her father's sheep shuffled forward to get water. Jacob stared at her with wide unbelieving eyes, as if in his great exertion he had lost all his social graces. It might have been that he had never seen a woman before, but it was rather that he had never seen what a woman could be to him, had never experienced another human being causing his throat to tighten as if he might suffocate, his insides to churn and contract, his thighs to weaken so that he feared he would not remain standing. He had never experienced another human being who created such yearning. Another. One who was not of him. A creature who had lived all her life in her own existence yet who seemed so immediately, so directly connected to him. A stranger whose pull was much greater than his pull over the stone had been. She looked up and her eyes burned into him, great depths, a look so strong and hard and *at him*. Connected. Mouth. Amused but soft, her lips pouting a gentle question at him. Body. Hidden, but here and there described by the concealing cloth, an outline, a sketch that suggested things Jacob had never yet got round to dreaming of. And her arms: rounded and downy. They might enclose him, as his had embraced the stone. His stone heart transformed into flesh by her touch. He might be enfolded in those arms, held against that body, those indistinct curves and hollows that spoke of softness and warmth and something else. All the unthought of, unimagined, unlonged for possibilities of encountering the physicality of a stranger came to him in that moment, standing and looking at Rachel. Her separateness was all promise of a doubling of himself, of making substantial what had become, during his hard lonely weeks in the desert, and perhaps had always been, depleted. Overwhelming loneliness was replaced like a flash flood with overwhelming wanting, with an immeasurable desire to be *together with*, and it was focused entirely on the beautiful and startling existence of the young woman who stood before him. Rachel. He walked towards her, not dreamily, but as if every fibre of his body was alert and strung taut, close to breaking point.

And Jacob kissed Rachel. Then, gasping at his temerity, he stood back. Now he wept. Hot tears spilled from his eyes and streamed down his face, streaking the dirt of his sunburned cheeks and drenching his dusty beard. Tears of he-did-not-know-what. He was weak, helpless, astonished. He knew nothing but felt everything, a pain, a sweetness and a gut-wrenching sense of future. As if he were being shaken by some interior mechanism, his whole body convulsed with the deep sobs that had been released by the touch of Rachel's lips on his. Behind him, the shepherds stopped laughing and were agog, finding themselves in the presence of something they did not understand, could not assess – a rare experience for them. Men had kissed women, men even had cried, but here was something disturbing and quite secret for all its being played out in public. They made themselves shrug, and soon they turned away in ones and twos, as if to get on with their evening conversation that had been interrupted.

Eventually Jacob got a hold on himself. The storm of tears died down, and he stood, muddy faced, loose shouldered, evis-cerated, it seemed to him, in front of Rachel whose eyes, beloved eyes, were wide with amazement. She had not moved, had not put a hand out to him, had not run away to the shep-herd lads, but just stood after receiving the kiss – an innocent touching of mouth to mouth, but tender, yearning in spite of his cracked, parched lips – and watched the stranger's tears fall. She was not embarrassed, but enchanted. No doubt that his tears were for her, though why exactly she could not say. She had had her effect on people all her life, but no one had ever wept for her, not like that, not as if he were shedding his whole being in order to remake himself for her and her alone. She shivered with the power of it. And what was more, beneath his mask of traveller's dust and weariness he was a striking man.

At last, he was in control of himself enough to speak.

'I am Jacob,' he said, holding out a hand towards her. Not apologising, not explaining. Simply introducing himself as he had omitted to do before he wept at the sight of her. 'We, you and I, are kin. I am Rebekah's son, your father's sister's son.'

She took his hand as he spoke and nodded, slowly absorbing what he was saying and what he was not saying. He was not a passing stranger. He had come to them. And the last time one of Abraham's line had come, he had married Rebekah. Rather, it was told in the family, Isaac had not come, but an emissary had been sent. This time, the bridegroom had come himself, not despatched a messenger. Rachel felt herself to be standing in the very place of her aunt Rebekah, standing by the well, receiving the promise of future, but this time with the groom himself, without concealment. Even his tears were on show. Her father, Laban, had been delighted with her aunt's marriage, with the bride price, anyway. This, then, was fitting, it had a precedent, it was possible, and it was like nothing that had ever happened to her before. Except, there was Leah. Older sister, unmarried. But Rachel looked again into Jacob's eyes and knew thrillingly that she had an ineradicable claim on his heart and soul.

Jacob followed Rachel back to her father's house where he was greeted like a long lost member of the family. Rachel raced ahead to tell of Jacob's coming and Laban ran out of the house and took him in his arms and welcomed him.

'My boy,' he said, holding him at arm's length and examining his nephew.

If there was a slight loss of light in his eyes as he first beheld

Jacob, tattered, desert-dirty and empty-handed, no entourage of camels, no gold bracelets, he quickly enough recovered himself when he saw his daughter's high colour and the way his nephew's eyes sought her out. He had heard tell that Abraham's son who had married his sister had done well for himself. It was a substantial branch of the family. Very substantial. Though why the boy was so dishevelled he could not understand. Young people. Things were different. He had much preferred woman-trading with Isaac's diplomatic emissary, dealing with important matters formally between people who understand the way of the world. Nevertheless, the lad looked strong and healthy. It would be another excellent connection in the new generation. Good to be well connected. As good as gold. You make a living any way you can. Family was important.

Jacob, the changed man, the man who had gone beyond the boundaries of family, crossing over from the silent tents of learning, from smoothness and cunning, from inaction, washed by exile and tears, now immersed himself in labouring on Laban's land. He rejoiced in his new physicality, working in the fields, breaking clods, mending tools, chopping wood, keeping watch over the flocks; he loved the new sense of the power under his skin and the release from the anxiety of thought. He was here as an exile. In hiding from the brother he had wronged – even if he had not been wrong to wrong him – paying for his disregard for the order of things with his hard labour. He discovered a love for the world outside the tent, for the speechless companionship of animal life that could be nurtured and increased, for the bite of the wind and the cooling sweat that ran down his face and shoulders. He was transformed. Still not his brother, not a man of the wilderness, but a man who fitted in to the scheme of things, who worked for its continuation and improvement. And he loved Rachel. Immeasurably. Several times a day she would pass him by on her errands, and he would stop what he was doing and simply watch and feel the overwhelming fact of his love for her. She waved at him, she smiled at him, she asked him at meals about life in Canaan. He was tongue-tied in her presence. Her power over him was too strong for words. He felt her, she lived inside him, at every minute of every day he knew she was there in the world. After the first kiss there had been no more, but that first kiss had not finished. Her mouth remained on his, a ghost mouth, pressed gently against his lips. He was overmastered by Rachel. Certainly she was beautiful and vibrating with life, but it was not how he thought of her. She was his Rachel, his destiny, the sum of his desire, the necessity of his life. Tears sprang again and again to his eyes as he revisited the memory of finding her in the world. Rachel was life.

'So, you seem to be staying with us. I wouldn't want your father to think I was exploiting my own kin. Tell me what you want in wages, my boy?'

It had become clear to Laban that Jacob was not just going to pay a bride price for his daughter and take her off back to Canaan. He showed no signs of leaving, or of making an offer. It dawned on Laban that Jacob *had* nothing to offer. Some trouble at home, he surmised. This was not what Laban had had in mind. Still, the lad was a good worker, a very good worker, and for a month he had laboured for nothing but his keep. No harm in having him around, he showed promise as a keeper of sheep. A small wage would keep him close until things were resolved with the family, and from the way the boy looked and sighed at Rachel, Laban was certain he wouldn't be asking for any very exorbitant pay to keep him hereabouts.

'I've got nothing, Uncle. But I will work for you for seven years in return for marriage to Rachel, your younger daughter.'

The deal was even better than Laban had hoped. A bright, able-bodied workman and potentially a fine stockman for seven years for nothing but food and clothing was a bargain he could not miss. As to Rachel, well, seven years was a long time. Something better might come up for her, for him, in the way of marriage offers, and in any case, by the time seven years had passed, surely Isaac and Jacob would have made up their differences. Jacob was a younger son, but Laban made enquiries and heard rumours about some deceit that had turned primogeniture on its head and given Jacob the right of inheritance. It wasn't the way of his people in this part of the world, but if it meant free labour and a good bride price, who was he to complain about the heterodox ways of the Canaanite branch of the family? He would worry about marriage and his girls when the seven years – or so –were up. A long time.

Let's pause the narrative for a moment to admire Laban. A fine example of practical humanity. Of man making a living. A businessman who knew that business was everywhere, that advantage was survival and comfort in a world where it was possible for a man to spend an entire life labouring from dawn to dusk and still have no more at the close of the last day than he had at the first. He had family, responsibility. Accumulation of goods, important contacts, influence abroad; these things made the difference. Opportunity was business: not to be missed and, if not available, to be made. He was fond enough of others, but not so that it fogged his mind as to his real purpose. Affection would not keep the family solvent and fed. Daughters were for marrying, contacts and bride price; nephews were for the same thing. And sheep were money, multiplying of their own free will and making more wealth for their owner. Like daughters, like sheep. It was a wonderful system, as long as you kept your wits about you. Laban was just an ordinary sort of man, getting by as best he could. And a kind of editor. A stitcher together of disparate narratives, a ruthless cutter out of anything that would hold up the progress and logic of the story. Though that, in this small aside, is precisely what I am doing. I hold things up – subvert my own purpose, if you like – just to point out that the editorial function takes many forms. Us managers of things, us behind the scenes tailors of reality are truly to be found everywhere.

Seven years *is* a long time. But for Jacob, distracted by love, they seemed no more than a few days. Everything he did was for the love of Rachel. Each getting up in the morning brought her closer and each settling down to sleep promised to whisk time away so that he might all the sooner have his heart's desire. Rachel was in each footstep, in each effort. Every lamb he heaved into the world, every sheep he saved from the jaws of predators, every stone he trudged over, was a sign of the coming of Rachel permanently into his life. Everything was nothing compared to that. He grew strong and knowledgeable. He watched the generations of sheep and goats and learned how to encourage the best and avoid the unwanted. The flocks multiplied and improved and he grew proud of his work. He delighted in being able to manipulate the world around him. He too was a sort of editor. So the time passed, hurrying by like the quick, light touch of Rachel's feet over the ground as she ran on that first evening to tell Laban of her cousin's arrival. Jacob considered all his labour and even his loneliness worth the prize he was aiming for. He watched Rachel, and over the years as she grew further into womanhood, his yearning for her increased.

There were women in the town who sold a snatched hour of their bodies, and Jacob made use of them, of course, but those moments were like washing or evacuating his bowels, nothing to do with his real life which would begin only when Rachel became his wife. Rachel was his meaning. She would make up for, would become, the family and the familiar homeland he had lost. He marked time, but used it well. Canaan receded into a past which seemed hardly to have existed. It was true that he never felt comfortable in Haran and that Laban and his family (Rachel excepted, Rachel always excepted) were no substitute for belonging in one's own place. He *was* lonely. He missed his texts. He missed his conversations with his teachers. He wondered about Esau and what he was making of his life, though never so much that he did not fear his sudden arrival, a late retribution from his womb-brother. There was no one to replace Rebekah and her harsh, practical view of the world. There was no one who loved him as fiercely as she did. No one, indeed, who loved him at all – though he had hopes that love for him was growing, secretly, in Rachel's breast. And even Isaac he missed, finding, oddly, that in spite of despising him as he had, there was a kind of fondness which seemed to grow with the years of absence. Nostalgia. A hankering after the past, after what had seemed to be the only way things could be – until he changed everything. A place and people who were forever just there, like it or not, but there where you had always been. He never lost his sense of strangeness in Laban's household.

But everything was worth the reward he was to receive. And Rachel, he believed, was growing to feel the same way. Nothing had been said, although Laban must have told her of the agreement he had made with Jacob. There was an understanding. Jacob did not just look at Rachel; Rachel looked at him. There were smiles of encouragement, at time looks of soft longing that were unmistakable. Sometime she would brush past him, so that he could smell the oils on her skin. The kiss was always there, he believed, special, between them. She continued her life and cared for her herd, laughing with the lads, though more circumspectly now as they had begun to marry.

It seemed that Laban was prepared to bide his time. A woman like Rachel could have married long before, but Laban put suitors off, told them to wait. A strong and clever nephew guaranteed to work for seven years and with important connections was worth more than a small bride price from some local fellow. But his girls were not getting younger and having two unmarried daughters was weighing heavily on him and on them.

Rachel found the years longer than Jacob.

'Don't worry,' Laban would soothe, as he did his accounts. 'He's worth waiting for.'

'Worth it for you or for me?' Rachel would ask sourly, knowing how her father calculated.

'We're family. What's good for me is good for you.'

'And in the meantime, I get older and dry up.'

'Nonsense, you are a beautiful woman and you're still hardly out of girlhood. You'll marry at your peak of desirability. These things go better when you're a little older. In no time you'll be the mother of a horde of children and you'll be wishing yourself unattached again.'

How much Laban knew about life. But Rachel saw the reason in it. She did not find it too hard to suppress her impatience. It wasn't clear to onlookers whether this was because her love for Jacob was as great as his for her and she therefore found time flashing past, or whether her desire was somewhat less and therefore more manageable. Jacob had no doubt. But others wondered.

For Leah there were no promises and no suitors. Nor was there reassurance from Laban. He had anticipated Leah's spinster-hood from an early age. It was a burden he supposed he had to shoulder. Spinsters in the family had their compensations as the parents grew older.

Although Leah had recognised Jacob as her childhood whis-perer and her intended husband, Jacob showed no signs of realising this. He was unfailingly pleasant to Leah. They even got on well. He spent time talking to her as he never did with Rachel. She was perhaps his only friend in Haran. She listened entranced to whatever he had to say because of the voice that was so familiar. But it never told her she was beautiful, and that she was his. On the contrary, he spoke of Rachel and of the lightning bolt that struck him at that first meeting, laughing at the strength he was able to summon to roll back the boulder. Leah understood what it was to be struck by a lightning bolt of love, so she listened with interest along with the anguish.

'She was so beautiful . . . but it was more than that.'

Nothing pained her more. Just being beautiful was not enough. Just! Even if Jacob could have perceived of Leah as a beauty, where and what was the 'more than that'? Yet how could his voice be so exactly the voice of her childhood champion if he and she were not meant to be together? Where was the sense in such a wonder with no purpose? Could wonders have no purpose just as ordinary everyday unsurprising life has none? Was the extraordinary just extraordinary and nothing more? Leah was unwilling to think so. Could one live and die a plain, unloved, childless woman and could there be no more purpose in Rachel being beautiful – as well as the 'more than that' – than just that fact? One plain, one pretty; fact, fact. No more to be said. But there was more. There were the open arms and indulgent laughter of the women as the child Rachel ran between them, and the open-hearted confidence to run about the world from there, to talk boyishly with the boys, to take her freedom, and 'more than that' which, if it existed, came either from the result of knowing she was beautiful, as if beauty was a wider road than plainness, or from those who perceived her and dug that wider road for her themselves. And Leah – better to have been born a boy, weak-eyed Leah? Not hideous, but without something; perhaps without the 'more than that' to start with that made a plain woman into an attractive one, or was it simply an unfortunate type and arrangement of features? Eyes too close together, too small, the face too long, the mouth too thin and too far below a hawkish nose. A pinched face with watery blue eyes that lacked shine. What made her her and Rachel Rachel? Now the disparity was a great gulf that allowed Jacob to talk to Leah and to love Rachel. Yes, she appreciated having a friend, albeit one who rarely turned the conversation in her direction, but the friend had the voice of one who had called her beautiful when she was small, who had promised her what had not seemed promising, and now, finding something better, had deserted her, except for friendship. Rachel was so firm in the world, she jostled the air with her presence, she was so sure of her right to displace it. Leah kept still and took up as little space as possible, allowing the air to sidestep her, to glide around her as if she were nothing more than an inanimate pebble on its way. Modest, dutiful, quiet, dull. That was Leah. These were qualities for which she was appreciated. She could be relied on when Rachel returned late from some jaunt and her herd needed watering. Rachel could rely on her, the family could rely on her, the sheep could rely on her. What if Rachel had been otherwise engaged on that day that Jacob arrived at the well and it had been Leah who had led the sheep from their pasture? Nothing. She knew nothing would have been different. Rachel would have come home and Jacob seen her later. Nothing would have changed. What was, was. Apparently.

One evening Leah came across Jacob walking slowly around the courtyard, as he often did once the lanterns had been lit and Rachel had retired to her room. She fell in thoughtful step with him, and he gave her a sideways smile. A small smile.

'You look sad?' she said.

'I've been thinking of home, remembering.'

'Do you miss it? I can't imagine being so far from home and alone.'

'I suppose I do miss it. But I'll never go back.'

'Why?'

'I did something. Made a mistake. A sort of mistake. A mistake anyway because I had to leave and I can't go home.'

'Really? Perhaps it's been forgotten. What could you have done that was so bad?'

Leah smiled at such an idea. Jacob shook his head.

'I couldn't tell you. It was a betrayal.'

'You?'

A look of pain crossed Jacob's face. It was so easy to be far away and let people assume that you were a decent, righteous, hard-working and courageous person. Not so easy to forget what you had done and to fear that the look of friendship in everyone's eyes would die once the truth was known. To Leah, who was his friend above all, he wanted to tell the truth. He wanted to test his reality against her friendship.

'I feel bad about what I did, but I would do it again. I'm sure

I would. I don't think I was wrong, not the outcome, but I feel bad about keeping that part of me a secret. As if I am lying to you about who I am, and to me. Like I'm a fraud. An impostor. I don't like the person who did that, but it was me and even though it sent me away from my family, I don't doubt it was the right thing to do. In one way. In another . . . I am ashamed. That's the thing. A shame. A . . . disgust.'

Leah listened but it made little sense.

'What was so terrible? Did you kill someone?'

'Not physically. I tricked someone, two people. I played a game and won it, but something about it reminds me of your fa— Something in me I don't like . . .'

'Tell me.'

'It would be a relief.'

'Then tell me. How can it change my affection for you? Jacob?'

So he told her about Esau, about his boorish brother selling his birthright, about his mother's plan to take Esau's paternal blessing. Then he stopped and started again. He told her about tricking his dim and hungry brother out of his birthright and how he had only worried that he would be caught by blind and bedridden and despised Isaac impersonating his brother. With the telling of both versions, a passably accurate tale was told. Leah was silent. This cunning Jacob, this stealer of what was other people's, was quite a different character from the one she had known, so vulnerable to her beautiful sister, used by her father, lost in the world, and deeply loved by her. In Leah's mind, Jacob's fineness thickened, his texture roughened. He was still all the things she knew him to be, but he had other aspects, wants, greeds and resentments. He became more human and less beyond her reach.

She reached out to him and touched his arm.

'It's the way families are,' she said. 'It's always like that.'

'Is it?' said Jacob who could not tell if the dim light in Leah's eyes had dimmed further since his telling.

So time passed. Jacob had weathered into himself, stronger, his hair and beard growing speckled, his face creased around the brow and the eyes. So Jacob paid his penance, though who was to say that mere penance would satisfy his dispossessed brother? So he learned more about the ways of sheep and goats, but perhaps not people. So the time of his reaching his one consuming desire came close. And in the meantime what was newly known lay curled in Leah's mind and it grew daydreams of its own. Leah loved Jacob, she was his friend, but he was her only possibility of happiness, he had told her so when she was very young, and now he was here. Sometimes, even the plainest, most unconfident girl must grasp what she can. She spoke to her father.

'It must be seven years soon that Jacob has been with us.'

Laban nodded absent-mindedly.

'And time for Rachel to be given as a wife.'

'I suppose so. No need to mention the time to Jacob. No hurry.'

'There is a hurry. For some of us.'

Laban had a moment of surprise and looked at Leah. She was what she was. It had never occurred to him that she might have minded about being an unmarried woman. It was necessary to work with all one's might to take advantage of life where it was possible, but what was the point of minding about things you could do nothing about?

'Has someone . . .?'

'No, no one has. But sometimes one has to speak up for

113

oneself. It seems that everyone does it. Wouldn't it be better for you, Father, if both your daughters were married?'

'Of course, but . . .' He looked embarrassed. 'There are other things for a woman than being a wife. You can be useful around the place. We must all learn to accept the way things are.'

'But some people don't. Do you know about Jacob and his brother Esau?'

Laban narrowed his eyes.

'I've heard rumours.'

'More than rumours. Jacob told me. I'm sure he was right to do it because he is a much better man to inherit the name and wealth of Abraham than his brother who by all accounts is an ass. It was pure trickery, but sometimes trickery can be at the service of a better result in the world. Don't you think?'

'Ye-es, but . . .'

'Rachel will marry no matter what. Rachel is not the daughter of yours who has a problem.'

Laban looked at Leah long and hard, his mind beginning to calculate with the information he had been given. He felt a new respect growing for his oldest daughter. All his paternal teaching had not been wasted. Looks, as everyone knew, weren't everything.

Jacob had kept careful count. His body had ticked the days, months and years away. The passage of time roared in his ears, desire made wild circuits round his body finding no proper outlet. Laban had said nothing. Rachel had said nothing. It was enough.

'I want my wife. I've worked my time. I want to bed her.'

It was brusque to a father, but Jacob had long since lost any illusions about Laban's sensitive nature. It was urgent. Laban had better know that; had better understand man to man that Jacob's needs could no longer be ignored. And he had better receive the impression that Jacob would pack up and go if he didn't get what he wanted, what he had been promised. He must not give Laban the idea, however true, that nothing would tear him from proximity to Rachel and that he would work a thousand years if she was to be his at the end.

But Laban responded as ever like a pragmatic man.

'Yes, yes, your time is done. Quite right. You should be married. Even if the seven years are not quite up.'

'They are quite up.'

The marriage feast was planned, all the local family and notable people thereabouts who counted were invited; the finest (almost the finest, one had to consider the breeding programme) lambs were chosen for slaughter and prepared, the women pounded and kneaded and baked and sewed for the forthcoming wedding.

For the marriage night the feasting tent was dark and sultry, only a few lamps threw dim shadows against the walls and flickered around the platters of food and jugs of wine. The music was loud and the laughter was raucous. Only men attended the feast and their clannish response to a marriage was a kind of wildness that drowned out all social and emotional claims and permitted only the bawdiness of a wedding night. They sang, they danced, they stamped their feet and clapped their hands. For most of the time they forgot Jacob, and the bride waiting in the women's tent, but celebrated or commiserated with each other over the joys and sorrows of being a man, of shouldering all the responsibility, of putting up with the ways of women, of having one or more of your own to hold close in the night and find relief of a kind – and then the morning would come and oh-the-trouble-and-the-nagging. Jacob joined in the carousing, being one of the men, drinking and joking about his last moments of freedom, while in a secret place (as perhaps had been the case with many of the drunken men egging him on, at their first wedding night), impatient for his freedom to be lost, supporting the final wait with a yearning tenderness, a sweet ache, a sense that after this moment life was to be quite different and he would no longer be alone.

His head reeled with his inner and outer intoxication. Men clapped him on the back and hugged him with all the comradely sentiment that wine can muster. Laban held him to his bosom.

'My son. My new son. What a fine pair we make to run the family business. Stay with us, stay, and with your husbandry skills and my business acumen, we will have great wealth. Welcome to the family.'

And the laughter from the men rose to a concerted roar, which Jacob assumed was because he was already of the family, though as a joke it hardly merited such a response.

'Well, we'll see, Uncle,' he said, beginning to feel that the most pleasant effects of the wine had run their course. His head started to feel a bit murky, and the swaying of the tent was now competing with the churning of his stomach. 'Why is it so dark in here?' he asked, peering at Laban.

'Local tradition, my boy,' he smiled. 'Local tradition. Got to keep the lamps low so as not to embarrass the bride when she comes to you.'

Laughter again.

'And when will she come to me?'

'Soon, soon. Drink up. That's another local tradition.'

116

And the wedding guests emitted another communal wave of drunken mirth.

At the height of the revelry, with drums beating and pipes hooting and the men cheering as they formed a rough approximation of a pathway from the opening of the tent to the dimly lit place at the far end where Jacob stood, the sound of women's laughter grew closer until it reached the tent and merged with the cheering of the men into a great chant: 'Hah hah hah hah hah hah hah hah . . .' they thundered rhythmically as the heavily veiled bride stood for a moment at the opening of the tent and then took a step forward.

'My daughter is yours,' Laban roared above the chant.

'Hah hah hah hah hah . . .'

And he led her towards Jacob and put her hand in his.

'Hah hah hah hah hah hah hah . . .'

Jacob's head tumbled with wine and the joy of at last having his only and true beloved to hold. Her veil was too dense and the light too dim to see her face, and he moved to lift it so that he might kiss his new bride, but Laban placed his hand over Jacob's.

'No, you must not lift the veil. It isn't fitting for her modesty. The first night a bride's innocence and shame must be respected. It can be lifted only when you are alone in the dark. A pure young woman must be allowed to adjust to her new circumstance. Local tradition.'

'Hah hah hah hah . . .'

'Now take her to your room and we will continue our celebration.'

The bride quivered as he took her hand in his and led her gently through the crowing crowd out of the tent, through the ululating women outside and towards his room. It was pitch black. The lamps were not lit, and when he felt for them he could not find them. Local tradition had made certain of retaining the bride's modesty. He did not care. He embraced her and lifted the veil. He heard her gasp and felt her body tense as he moved close to her. He loved her all the more for her tremulousness. For the second time in seven years Jacob kissed his bride.

'My love,' he whispered, trying to push away the less pleasant effects of the wine he had drunk. Of all times, now was when he wished his head to be clear, his perceptions to be sharp. It was too late, he had drunk too much. But nothing could detract from the great expanse of peace and contentment that surged through him as he let his hands slide over the rough linen and smooth silken wedding robes, and felt the firm, vibrating life underneath his palms. 'At last. My love. My beautiful Rachel.'

'Yes, I am, I am your Rachel,' his bride murmured as their loosed wedding clothes fell in a dark pool on the floor and their hands encountered the new-found bodies that were now to be joined together for life. For *life* was exactly how Jacob felt it. He was forgiven and as a sign of his redemption he had the smooth curves and soft declivities of his beloved beneath his adoring fingers, her scent, the oils he knew only from a distance, the feel of her loosened thick swathes of hair in his hands and curtaining him as he lay beneath her receiving her kisses, released at last, and astonishingly free from the modesty of an unmarried girl. She was passionate as he had never known in the women he had paid to keep him from going mad while he waited for his love. Her desire was at least the equal of his and it led her, as she led him, to a night of profound exploration of pleasure and finally, finally, and then again and again, release. They lay together saturated with each other, exhausted, astonished, wasted, gasping for air and longing for a breath of a breeze to cool their overheated slippery bodies, but clinging to one another nonetheless with promises of love and happiness and passion to come, never to stop, on and on. Each other's.

'Rachel – my wife.'

'Jacob – my husband.'

Jacob slept until the dawn had begun to brighten the darkness and erase the shadows. For a few moments, he lay watching the rosy tinge inside his closed eyelids deepen to a stronger crimson. It was a special perverse pleasure to keep his eyes shut just for a second, and a second longer, putting off the delicious moment when he chose to open them and would see, for the first time and for the rest of his life, his wife, his beloved Rachel, lying beside him.

Leah had not slept at all. There was too much to remember of the previous night and too much to anticipate of the coming dawn. Her open eyes peered into the darkness and then noted its slight alleviation, and all her nerves went on alert, ready for the moment when Jacob's head would turn in her direction and he opened his eyelids. The dark had served its purpose, so well, remarkably well, but now the approaching dawn would tear away the veil that night had substituted for the one she had let drop heart-flutteringly to the floor. A lifetime of hope had been realised that night for Leah. While it happened it was enough – or rather it was everything. But now, as she lay waiting for the rising sun to tweak Jacob into consciousness, she wondered about the rest of her life, about the nights beyond the single, almost perfect one that had just passed.

'Rachel,' Jacob breathed. Leah had already sensed the

beginning of his growing awareness. He rolled his head away from the light breaking through the woven cloth at the window to face his wife, and opened his eyes.

Leah held his empty stare without blinking. The set of his face showed nothing, except that the blood and the effects of the sun and wind drained away, leaving a pale parchment tone to his skin, untouched by the beams of dawn. He looked; Leah looked steadily back. They were close enough for even her poor eyes to see him with perfect clarity. The momentary shock that flooded his eyes as he opened them and saw her, gave way to puzzlement – perhaps he wasn't awake, but yes he was – and then a searching look that went right beyond her face, while the night replayed in his mind, and he realized, Leah supposed, what had happened, and why it was that she and not Rachel was in his bed that dawn. But still he said nothing. Leah watched him with such intensity that his face seemed to break up into separate planes, his forthright familiar face, so solid and broad, became in their locked gaze just a series of intersecting slants of angled flesh, degrees of contours, shades of pale, like a familiar word that is repeated over and over until it becomes entirely strange. He stared and continued to stare, and when the thoughts had run their course, when, Leah imagined, he understood that this was not a dream, not a joke – no one was laughing, not now, not now that the deed was done and irreversible, and that no pause of his was going to replace Leah in his bed and through the previous night with Rachel, and that a marriage had been performed, his marriage to her, to Leah – Jacob rolled away from her on to his side, quite slowly, and rose from the bed. He picked his robe from the tangle of clothes on the floor and pulled it around himself, then left the tent without glancing back. He had not spoken a word, nor made a sound. And in the enduring silence Leah gazed at the empty air he had left in the doorway.

Laban was the worse for wear, but did not know it since he was still asleep when Jacob flung open the door of his room. He was not alone, a favourite concubine was curled up beside him, sweetly and silently asleep in spite of the snores and grunts of her master. If she woke when Jacob began cursing at his uncle, she showed no signs.

'What have you done to me?' Jacob cried at Laban who started, tried to grasp to the echo of his nephew's words, remembered, and realised that such an awakening this morning had been inevitable. Groaning with the pain inside his head and the argument to come, he made a supreme effort and opened his eyes.

'Ah, my beloved nephew and son-in-law, Jacob.'

'You deceived me. Why did you do this to me? It was Rachel, you knew it was Rachel I loved, Rachel I served you seven years for. You gave me Leah. Leah! How could you trick me like this!'

Even with the deep sobs that constricted his throat, Jacob managed to throw his words out like spears, fighting back the shock and tears of rage that had shaken him since leaving his marriage bed. Laban sat up and began a shrug and then stopped because of the extra pain it caused at the back of his head. He waited for a moment to make sure Jacob had finished.

'My boy, in our part of the world it is not done to give the younger child precedence over the firstborn. It's not the way of civilized people. Anyway, since it's only now that you complain, it would seem that in the dark you did not notice *who* you were married to. Your sense of hearing and of touch weren't acute enough to inform you of the truth of who was in your bed, eh? Strange, when the girls are so different. Perhaps your hunger was too great. Perhaps true love and rough appetite are closer than you thought. Love turns out to be less pure and simple than you imagined, eh?'

Jacob shut his mouth, swallowing the corrosive taste of injustice and despair that rose up through him. A picture flashed across his mind of his blind and bedridden father reaching out his hand, and the tearfully enraged threats of vengeance from Esau. And a look in Laban's eye said that he knew of them too. Quite the moral teacher Laban turned out to be, though actually he was, of course, more of a gleeful opportunist. Jacob, however, was momentarily silenced, whatever the source of the lesson. But on the other hand, he was married to the wrong woman. He was now committed to a woman he did not love. Whom he did not desire. Who, in a thousand years and a world empty of women, it would never have crossed his mind to marry. His whole life was altered – no, *destroyed*. What had happened between him and Esau was not at all the same. There was a higher rightfulness about that. This was mere and mean trickery. As if Laban heard his thought, he smiled through his headache, highly amused.

'Well, if you find last night's pleasures are this morning spoiled by the sight of a plain woman, never fear, I've given her Zilpah as her servant. A pretty little thing.' He turned slowly to look at the girl lying beside him and stroked her sloping thigh under the quilt. 'And with delightful attributes.' He saw the rage wind up in Jacob. 'However, I'm a reasonable man: just finish the bridal week of this wife – do your duty, boy – and in return for a further seven years' service, we'll give you the other one – on account, this time. You can have her in just one week.

You see how I trust you to fulfil your side of the bargain? Can't say fairer than that, can I? Two for the price of . . . two.'

But Jacob was already disappearing through the doorway by the time Laban had finished making his offer. He returned to his room where Leah was now robed and sitting at table drinking sweet morning tea. When he threw open the door she looked up at him as boldly as her myopic eyes could, and imagined, if not actually saw, his look of hatred and contempt.

'You did this. It wasn't just him. Laban couldn't have done it without your consent. Without your treachery. You were my friend. My only friend. I thought you were honest. How could you do this to me? You know I love Rachel. Only Rachel. I thought you cared for me.'

'I did care for you. I do care for you. Do you think you're the only one who loves?'

'But you lied to me. How could you do that? All night in my arms. There in that bed in the midst of making . . . I called out Rachel's name to you as I . . . what we did . . . what happened last night. I called out "Rachel" and you answered me. You said, "Yes." You said, "Yes, I'm your Rachel." Is that love?'

'Oh, yes it is. I love you so much I became Rachel for you. And you loved *me* last night as you loved Rachel. It was only this morning that you noticed I wasn't her; does that make our night together – your pleasure and passion – disappear? Does that make your love for me last night any less? I will be anything I have to be for you. I can be Rachel, or better still I can be me. Last night, whether you knew my name or not, it was me you loved. Here's the thing: I love you. Do you think Rachel loves you like I do? Who knows who Rachel loves?'

'But you tricked me. You pretended to be someone you were

123

not—' He stopped short at the sound of his own words and the harsh laugh that came from Leah.

'What a lot we have in common, my cousin, my husband. When your father called out to Esau in his darkness, didn't you answer him in Esau's name? You will come round to loving me, like you loved me last night.'

Jacob turned away, his lips pressed tightly together. To think he had imagined this daughter of her father to be his friend. How could she have used what he had told her, his most private secret, how could she have used it against him, and present it to him now in crowing triumph? And she betrayed his confidences to her father. The treachery overwhelmed him. However much the darts hit home about his own betrayals and deceits, he could not feel that he deserved this much punishment. For him there had been some justification, but this . . . To trick him into marrying a wife he did not love, a wife he did not desire, to have and to hold for ever. An enemy, now, for a wife. Even if he *was* going to have Rachel too – and another seven years of hard labour for his wretched, grasping uncle – it would still never be the same as having her alone, his true, his first and only bride. Nothing was going to be the way he imagined it. If he *had* worshipped and cried out over Leah's body, it had been in the belief that it was Rachel he was adoring, pleasing and getting pleasure from. Just because he howled in ecstasy in the dark did not mean that he would have done so in the light. In the dark, in the imagination, things are what they seem to be, what they are supposed to be. That does not make them the truth. Leah, as she said, *was* Rachel, that night. From now on and in retrospect, however, she would be Leah, known and forever loathed for her deceit, for the advantage she had taken of the blindness of his love. How could she imagine he would ever love her? Plain, pinched, feeble-eyed Leah, a good enough friend (or so he had thought) but never, not in his wildest imaginings, a lover or a beloved. It could never be. If she had to be his wife, so be it. It did not mean she had to be loved. Indeed, it did not mean she any longer even had to be liked.

He shook his head at her in disgust. No cruelty could be too great for what she had done. He spoke with careful clarity.

'You must know this, be absolutely sure of this: I will never love you, Leah. I may have to be your husband, but in a week Rachel will be my true wife. I will love her and only her until I die, and you can wither like desert grass for all I care. Yes, I have a duty to you now. I can't escape it. It is done. I will do what is my duty. You will be fed and clothed and housed. But you will never be loved. Rachel is beautiful, graceful, a force of life – all things you will never be. What would you be loved for? You aren't even as loyal as a dog. Rachel will always be my love. You will remain unloved.'

Leah kept her face blank and replied after a moment in a strained whisper.

'Don't you see what I have sacrificed to prove my love for you?' she said, lowering her head, speaking to her lap. 'I have risked everything. Isn't that proof of the power of what we could have between us? Rachel will never love you like that. She can't, she gazes too deeply at her own reflection. What you love in Rachel, what she may or may not love in you, will pass. Then you'll have only a memory, a dead love. Don't you want to be loved as no one else could ever love you?'

'Not by you. I'd rather be hated by Rachel than loved by you. Remember this: I hate you. Your husband, your only husband, who will do whatever his duty is insofar as he has to, does not and will never love you, but loathes the sight of you, abominates the very ground you walk on, the sound of your breath, the scent of your skin. You will only ever be vile to me. That's what you have gained by your trickery.'

Leah breathed in slowly as if taking his words into her deepest place, her pallid tender eyes fogging behind cloudy film.

'That is much less than you gained by yours,' she whispered.

She had never been beautiful. Her long heavy-jawed face with its ill-proportioned features had never caused a light to flare in other eyes. At best she had the indignity of pity, most of the time she simply wasn't noticed. Someone had to be like that, to be ordinary enough to get the chores done, not to be a dreamer but to be a help in the daily business of keeping a household going. That was what unmarriageable girls were for. They had their uses. But she had had her dreams. Quiet private dreams which had convinced her that there was some way she could be seen, really seen, by the right person. Where had she got such a notion? She had waited. She believed that a man would one day look at her and a light would dawn in his eyes, a sudden softening into realisation of what she was, what she could be. A seeing into her, not just a glancing over her face and body that happened when men looked at Rachel and needed delve no further into her qualities before they were smitten. Jacob was smitten by Rachel. Love was something else. As an unloved woman, Leah knew this. She had to know it. It grew, it came as an understanding, a dawning. No, she wasn't pretty or vibrant, but there would be someone who would see what she actually was. That she was clever, tenacious, loyal – yes, loyal in a true sense – and with an understanding of the world and what was important. Also, that she was beautiful. If you looked at her rightly, she had beauty, too. And it had to be Jacob who finally really saw her. Once she had seen him and heard his voice, it could be no one else.

What had she gained by her trickery? Jacob as a husband. Time for him to learn to love her, to grow aware of her qualities. And if she hadn't reckoned with her father also giving Rachel to Jacob, unable to resist another free seven years of his labour, it didn't matter. Let him have her as a second wife. Soon enough the obvious would pall and he would begin to see which sister had the capacity for love and companionship. Rachel could not sustain a man's love over the time of a marriage, a lifetime. And already love had shown Leah (and Jacob when he finally realised) something that neither she nor anyone else had dreamed about herself. Last night in Jacob's arms, in the dark, she had discovered a physical equivalent to the yearning in her heart for her beloved. A gift for passion had been revealed, a physical understanding of desire that she had not known she had. Her body took to sexual pleasure instantly, understood what it wanted and how to encourage it. And it understood also how to give pleasure, how bodies might be smitten by another's touch, by each other's touch, and how the play of touch and smell and taste and sound stoked the fires that suddenly flared up so brightly in her. How all the senses could take and give and combine with another to build to an ecstasy, an overflowing of the body and mind engaged with another. She had no shyness, no fear of caressing and being caressed, everywhere, everything, no sense except that what they did together and to each other was an essential part of the entire business of love in the world. He gasped at what she did to him, and both were astonished at how confident and accomplished a lover she was. When they finally lay in the dark in each other's arms, drained of all energy, they were filled with wonder and delight that love could be so

127

much and that this was yet only the very beginning. Poor, plain Leah was made for love. How would she have ever learned that about herself if she had not tricked Jacob? And how could Jacob, having experienced it, not come to realise the absolute and blinding truth of their love?

All Jacob could think about was the six days and nights he had to get through before Rachel was finally his. The seven years had been nothing, but these extra seven days moved with infinite slowness as if the sun and moon had aged and could barely manage to creep around their circuits in the sky. The days ached to end, the nights longed for dawn. The whole world around him seemed to be waiting gasping for the passing of those lengthy lingering seven days. The requirement of a new husband was that he spent the wedding week sleeping with his wife, while the feasting and gaiety went on around. It ensured, it was said, the coming of the first child, the portent of many more to come, both beddings and feastings. Jacob abided by the letter of his obligations. Grimly, and very late, he came to bed with Leah, his day's work done, having eaten alone and walked around his herds until it was impossible to stay upright any longer. She was never asleep, but always silently turned back the cover for him. He said nothing. He had said all he wanted to say to Leah. He slept instantly, keeping a careful empty space between them. Leah woke him sometimes, touching him, caressing his body, trying to warm the memory of their passion, or at least incite his ordinary manhood.

'I did my duty by you on our marriage night. Leave me alone.'

'You did your duty by Rachel that night. Now do your duty by me.'

'Since you took me for a fool, you must take what you can get.'

'But what of the pleasure we gave each other?'

'That was when you were Rachel. Now you are Leah.'

'How will I conceive?'

'Rachel, my wife Rachel will conceive. I am not interested in your children.'

'A woman must have children.'

'A woman must have children by the right husband.'

His unbending harshness left her weeping every night, and Jacob was not sorry as he fell asleep to the sound. There was not a glimmer of pity. An old self-righteous hardness rose in him, the same quality – his very own quality though there were others – that permitted him to take the birthright from his help-lessly dull-witted brother for just a handful of lentils. Whatever the echoes of his own deceptions, they could not for him cancel out a burning sense of outrage at this grasping deceit, at the ruination of his life by uncle and cousin. Jacob's assault on the expectations of Esau's life had been just as devastating, just as lifelong in its repercussions, but in that case there had been a greater justice involved, a matter of fitness: Jacob's clear fitness over Esau that made his trickery essential if unfortunate. Though there was a lesson to be learned from what had just happened to him, and he regretted the pain he now realised he had caused Esau, he didn't doubt its necessity. Leah, on the other hand, had wanted nothing but her own selfish desires. She had deprived him of a lifetime of singular domestic bliss with his only beloved and the woman who was clearly intended by fate or God (it didn't matter which) to be the mother of the seed of Abraham. Leah was not fitter than Rachel to be his wife, indeed, she would have been no one's wife had she not lied her

129

way into his bed. Well, if she wanted so badly to be his wife, she had what she wanted. That was all she would get. Somehow, he and Rachel would ignore his first wife. They would weave a cocoon of love to wrap their lives together and have their rightful destiny – growing old as they watched the new generations of the children of Abraham thrive.

It is not for editors to be astonished by their subjects. They are what they are; an opinion is not called for. Like the Creator, we discover what we have got and work with it, shape it, make it, within the constraints of the materials we are given, as clear as possible, as orderly and reasonable as the mess we've been handed can be moulded to become. And also like Adam's Maker and Abraham's Shield we are rendered silent by the very voices – less adept than us but louder in their own sphere – that are nothing until we breathe life and sense into them. Well. Not, of course, that we don't have beliefs and opinions, and though it might be said that it is our job to keep them to ourselves, it would be unreasonable to expect no response at all from those of us who cut and paste and make artefacts of chaos. Human love and unreason dealt the blow to the God of Abraham: *I am that I am* skulked behind silence, rejected by and infected with humanity. Well, there are other ways to skin a cat. *I am that I edit*. Better to edit than to create. Less rejection, less infection. Keep an underhand on the narration and control will take care of itself. Story is everything to them; well then, control the story.

But, my, how love, human love (what other kind is there?) trips us overarching ones up. What rational, editorial being could have imagined such a thing? What could the woman have been thinking of? Not a stupid woman. How little experience of

130

that aspect of life do you have to have not to know that *you cannot make another human being love you?* Marry you, yes. Be tied up – grimly, virtuously, resignedly – with your existence for as long as existence is, yes. But love, no. About love, like humans themselves, there is nothing to be done. Yet Leah, a woman who knew the shadows and intransigence of life well enough, felt her love for Jacob so powerfully it was inconceivable to her that, given the opportunity to experience it, he should not love her back. Such a flowering of certainty, such a burning focus, such a burden simply could not go unreciprocated. She allowed that he was not stricken by her as he had immediately been by Rachel, and as Leah had been by him, but loving him as she did, she was convinced that his love for her was therefore a necessary eventuality. A thing that had only to be realised by him for it to blossom into what it already was. Love such as she experienced, longing such as she had concentrated on the being of Jacob could not possibly be unrequited. How, she thought, can he not love me once he realises he does? The bizarre logic of love. *How can he not love me?* Editors may be forgiven for pausing briefly to shake their heads before carrying on with their thankless, baffling task.

He did not love her. He continued not to love her. He did not touch her again during the wedding week, and then, after a somewhat subdued second wedding – barely a meal, let alone a feast – when Rachel finally became Jacob's bride, Leah saw him only from a distance, in passing. He did not glance at her. He did not speak. She had become invisible, quite slipped from any world in which he lived. She had her servant, Zilpah, and the company of the other women, as she always had, but now not only was there no voice of promise whispering in her ear, there was no hope either. Leah's life in the early days of her marriage went on just as her life before it, all she had gained was a lifeless memory of what might have been, or – some immediately suppressed thought suggested – what never could have been.

Rachel seemed pleased enough with her married condition. Love suited her, it always had. She seemed to grow lusher and more beautiful with every passing night. She would greet Leah when they met with a sisterly smile, and something else behind it that made Leah's head reel. Had Leah always been jealous of Rachel? Perhaps not. Perhaps early on she hadn't understood the power over life that Rachel possessed merely by looking as she did. Certainly, Leah grew to despise her sister, with her easy access to affection and the interest of others. A smile, a wriggle, a pout. She deemed her shallow, thoughtless and eventually doomed. She looked around her at the older women of the household, and she saw clearly that beauty and youthful energy fade, and that the certainty of self which is so compelling to others fades also as these props disappear. That was evident. There were older women among the household and servants who looked as if they had once been beautiful. Their faded beauty and their memories of what once had been and was no longer, turned down the corners of their mouths, dragged at their eyes and wearied their flesh more, it seemed to Leah, than their plainer sisters who had grown into themselves, become what they would become, and who watched those who had been what they once were lose the sparkling confidence with which they once owned the world. Leah concluded that in the long run . . . but yes, Leah had always been jealous of Rachel. These comforting thoughts about the effects of time were retrospective. Youth, to the plain young as well as the pretty young, goes on for ever. Age is inconceivable as anything more than something that some people, not oneself or one's peers, already are. And even if she managed to imagine Rachel's future ruined looks and habit-induced ordinariness, it held no compensation for the disparity in the present lives of the two girls. Leah had to come to terms with being a useful and valued member of the household and watch her sister prance – was it with deliberate cruelty, with a knowing glance backward at her older sibling? Of course, Leah felt it like that. But in all likelihood, and far worse, it was just the carelessness of the joyful, of a life full of love and laughter. A lack of thought was Rachel's worst crime, a failure to be both-ered to imagine what it might be like to be Leah and have a sister like Rachel. But why would she think such painful thoughts about her sister, whom she loved? It was Leah who looked at the other and imagined what it was like to be her. Thoughtfulness is born of time to think. Rachel was too busy with enjoyment to think such thoughts.

'Are you happy?' Leah asked Rachel in the early days of her marriage when they sat together preparing food for their hus-band and it was still possible to pretend a sisterly fondness for each other.

'Of course,' Rachel smiled vaguely. It did not occur to her to ask her sister the reciprocal question.

'Do you love him?'

Rachel looked up, startled.

'Well, of course. He's my husband. Don't you love him?'

'Yes, I love him.'

'There then,' she returned to her bread-making. 'Sometimes I miss herding the sheep. I miss meeting up with the lads and the chatter. But Jacob's right, you can't be a mother and a shep-herd at the same time.'

'You're pregnant?' Leah whispered faintly.

'Will be.' Still, she didn't ask the reciprocal question.

'He doesn't love me. He doesn't touch me.' Leah's voice was barely audible.

'What? Oh. Well, you did trick him into marrying you. It's not the best way to win a man's love. I'm sure he'll grow fond of you. And at least you're married. Settled. You know? And we're sisters. You've always got me. We're family. I'll make sure he does right by you. He'll do anything I say. He's mad for me.'

Leah dropped her head as she pounded her dough and folded her tears into it. She wondered if Jacob would notice any difference between the two loaves he ate that night?

Jacob had his true wife at last. His only wife, he decided. He would put Leah to the back of his mind, and his existence. He would do no more than fulfil his obligations to her: feed her, keep her. It was better than she might have expected had she not tricked him into marrying her. Rachel filled his life and his mind. As far as he was concerned their first night together was the first night of his married life. He took his treasure by the hand and led her into his tent. This time the lamps were lit, he had made sure of that, and when he lifted her veil – there were no concessions to maidenly modesty – he breathed a sigh of relief that it was indeed Rachel, his true wife, beneath it. Then he sighed the fullness of his heart.

'My love, my only love,' he whispered.

'Have you not come to love my sister?' She teased, giggling.

Jacob put his finger to her lips.

'We will not speak of her. She does not exist for us. You are my love, my only love. You are all I have ever wanted in the world.'

He led her to bed and this time he was trembling. Rachel smiled her loveliest most distant smile, her lowered lashes sparkled as her half-shut eyes picked up the gleams in the lamp-light, and she stood modestly waiting as Jacob undressed her and stroked her naked body with hands that over the past seven years had learned to reassure the most fearful and fragile new-born lambs in his care. He laid her carefully on the bed and, slipping out of his robe, stretched out beside her. He touched her cautiously as if she were a fragile object. Though she was fleshier, lusher than her sister, it was as if she were a delicate engraving on fine eggshell. He seemed to himself too heavy, too clumsy for her not to complain of the weight of his love. He resisted his own powerful desire to enclose her in a binding grip and to let the full crushing intensity of passion engulf her. He feared the enormity of his own need, and so took the greatest care of her in the storm of love that raged inside him and threatened to overwhelm them both. This was the real thing. A worshipful love, a love that shimmered in the light. That, he saw, was the difference between lust and love.

It was a long awaited night of love. A culmination of hopes and dreams. She murmured sweetly and kissed his neck, she held him, perhaps a little at a distance, in her embrace when he shuddered to his climax. Rachel was at last his lover – not exces-sively demonstrative, not knowing, not overcome with pent-up desire – if he felt that there was a certain withholding, it was to be expected of a virgin who would be gently led to the further reaches of passion as her modesty was overcome. If he was constrained by her passivity, so that he did not explore the full range of the questions his body asked about her, well, there was a lifetime for them to learn the intimacy and power of their wanting. Not everything happens all at once. And anyway, he thought in sleepy confusion for the merest second before he expunged the memory, they had already had the most profoundly passionate love together that first night, when he had loved his Rachel and she him, utterly and perfectly, so perfectly, in the dark.

Some weeks later, Jacob was working in the fields with Laban's sheep, examining the lambs for signs of disease, when he saw a woman walking towards him in the distance. His heart jounced. Rachel had not been out to visit him in the fields since they were married. He'd suggested she come, that she keep up her shepherding skills by spending some time with him and the flocks, but she hadn't shown any interest. He was excited at the idea of sharing what he did and what he'd learned with his beloved Rachel. There remained a sort of distance between them, no easy familiarity had yet emerged. Rachel took pleasure in Jacob's devotion to her, and Jacob was daily astonished that she should be his wife, and that he should be so freely permitted to be devoted to her. But there was no domestic ease between them. Perhaps, Jacob thought, there was too much love for that. If their life together was quite formal, it was because love structured their every moment. But still a powerful excitement, and a sense of relief broke over him at the sight of Rachel approaching to join in his regular world of fields and sheep.

Quite soon, however, he realised it was not Rachel coming towards him; the figure lacked the boldness, the spring in the step, and her head was down, looking at the soil. It was not Rachel's way of going about the world. She looked always up and around her. He saw, the leap of his heart turning immediately into a tightening knot of anger in his chest, it was Leah. He did not want to see her, certainly not speak to her, here where he was most with himself. They had not had a private conversation since the morning after they were married. He would not have her interfering in his life.

'Jacob, my husband.' Her words were insistent but her voice was small. She continued to look down, for fear of seeing the animosity in his eyes.

'What? What are you doing here?'

'I have news.'

'Has something happened to Rachel . . .?'

Leah felt Jacob's sudden burning interest. He moved towards her, almost reached out. She shook her head fast.

'No, no. It's my news.'

She looked up but Jacob's face immediately closed again against her and his hands dropped to his sides.

'I'm not interested in your news. You must leave me alone. I do not want to have anything to do with you beyond what is necessary. There is nothing between us.'

'I'm pregnant,' Leah said, without emphasis but holding her ground and looking now directly at him with her weak, watery eyes.

His response was instantaneous.

'You can't be. How can you be, when we have never . . .'

Then a moment of appalled silence. Just the idiot jarrings of the sheep and the tinny echo of the lambs. Jacob and Leah heard only the sound of their own blood rushing in their ears. In that instant before his sentence died, Jacob was quite certain that he had never spent a night with Leah, that they were married in name only, and that he had never touched her as a man touches a woman. She was a stranger to him. The night of the wedding had come to belong to Rachel, to a dream of Rachel that had come in his mind actually to be her. He had managed to expel Leah entirely from the memory of that night. But the stark reality of Leah standing unmoving, her pale eyes staring and half-open mouth gasping at his words, challenging him to deny her, broke through finally into Jacob's consciousness and prevented his sentence from finishing itself.

'I am carrying your child,' Leah said quietly and turned away.

Jacob watched her walk back across the field.

When he got back that evening, Rachel was not in their rooms. Jacob called her maid, Bilhah, to him and asked where she was.

'She has gone to wait out her time of uncleanliness in the women's quarters,' Bilhah told him, her young cheeks flashing red with embarrassment at having to speak to a man of such things.

Leah had Jacob's firstborn, a son, whom she named Reuben. The gestation and birth were easy; it seemed that Leah was made for childbearing. The sharp edges of bone under stretched skin softened as pregnancy rounded her out, her long face lost its melancholy cast and even her short-sighted glare took on a warmth that transformed it into a kind of misty contentment. Leah flowered in her pregnancy. Even before it quickened, she could actually feel life starting and growing inside her, saw in her mind and experienced in her body the long-dried seed that had at last been watered, begin to live. She could feel the new existence developing inside her, saw it with an inner eye, touched it with an inner hand that was perfectly attuned to the workings of her interior processes. She delighted in being the growing medium of life. Though her eyes suffered even more from short-sightedness as the pregnancy went on, she welcomed the child with every breath she breathed during its development. She carried herself differently too. She held her head up as she went about her business in the world. Her tread was firmer, her shoulders were higher, lighter. She was with child. With Jacob's child. His firstborn would be born to her, to Leah, the despised wife and sister. She did not have to throw triumphant glances at Rachel. It was only too clear how healthily and happily pregnant Leah was. And if Rachel took Leah's continual smile as victorious, it was not really intended. Leah simply could not help smiling. She had only to look down at her swollen belly for her smile to spread across her face. But of course Leah *was* victorious, she had won life, and at last of the two disparate sisters it was she who had the advantage, the only advantage in their world that mattered.

She held the squalling child in her arms after the birth. Now. At last. After all the suffering, this. A boy, wriggling and wailing great breath-and-life-filled cries in her arms. Her boy, her child. Her son with Jacob. The pain, the sorrow, of her life was over. It was all but forgotten in the wonderment of her new fortune, and certainty of a quite different future. Her life was changed. Everything was changed. Now, she whispered to her newborn boy, to Reuben son of Jacob, now I have had his firstborn. Now my husband will love me.

Ancient Jacob, the old man broken by the loss of his beloved son, his true firstborn, Rachel's child, Joseph, wept noisily and tore at his clothes from dawn to dusk and through the long hours of the dark, mourning far beyond the time when it is considered right for a grieving father to collect himself, return to the world and acknowledge again those who remain among the living. But his cries continued to ring through the house and compound so that the tragedy of Joseph's death was experienced minute by minute by all those who lived and worked within its boundaries. Jacob rarely left his rooms, but when he did it was to glare at those around him who went about their daily business, as if all activities should have ceased with the loss of his treasured boy. He stared hatefully at the sight of his other sons tending the sheep or maintaining the crops – let them starve, let them rot, what could any of it matter now? Why should anyone care about the future? He had no further interest in posterity. He looked scornfully at the women preparing and cooking food, mending clothes, weaving cloth. How could such things go on? How could new cloth be woven when clutched in his hand day and night he held the bloody fragment of the garment his son had been wearing when he was torn to pieces by a wild beast? Let new cloth be forbidden, let the sheep sweltering in their unsheared wool be savaged, every one, their entrails torn out by the same deadly creature that had taken his beautiful boy. Let the other sons, the unloved wife who lived on solely as a bitter reminder of his dreadful losses, the concubines, their children and their children's children dry up and shrivel. How dare those around him flaunt life when death was all there was left in the world? Even Benjamin, the lastborn, his late joy and sorrow, could not console him.

How long had he waited for that child, for Rachel's firstborn to arrive? What had he gone through? Back then, the time before the begetting of Joseph, he was like a man who had lost sight of the rising and setting sun, a creature without direction, without any will of his own. After the seven years of promise, the working towards his dream, the perfect fulfilment he expected had been smeared by trickery, by complexity. His one love, his single love and life had been muddied with an unwanted woman and then her unwanted, but needed children. He watched his dream of happiness sour and disintegrate as it and he were buffeted between the more powerful dreams of happiness of the women. His spirit declined while he went about his life, apparently normally. There was not the slightest sense that anything or anyone was 'with him' or he with them or it. He echoed like an empty jar. He became a remnant blown by the emotional winds of others over whom he seemed to have no control. Like now. What could he do about his lost son? What could he have done caught up in the whirlwind storms of the women who in their attempts to better each other had pulled his own life out from under him and crushed his will? So much hope for seven years, a new-found real existence to work towards, and then, so much strife and disappointment. If Rachel did not appear to love Jacob as he loved her, or to be content, it was because of Leah, he had no doubt. Not that Rachel didn't love him, but she had no time or energy to devote to love amid the rivalry and anger against her sister. It was Leah's fault if Rachel and Jacob did not have the idyllic equality of love that he was convinced should have been theirs. And where was the God of Abraham? Where was the promise that made him more than the sorry creature his father had become? Where was his *size* in a life devoted to working for another man and being a pawn between two angry women? And then the first catastrophe, the great love lost, his Rachel, his beloved, just as easefulness seemed within reach. And following that blow, this: the wonderful child, his joy and hope for a contented-enough old age snatched from him, right under the criminally careless eyes of his other sons, by the whim of a wild animal. Once again Jacob was a featherweight buffeted helplessly by life's cruelty. If not his wives, then wicked chance conspired to keep him from his rightful condition of a successful, contented elderly man basking in the happy results of his past and knowing that the future and his memory was secure. And where was the Lord, the Lord of the lofty promise? 'I will be with you.' Where had he been each time these vicious stones were thrown at him and hit their mark? Had this Lord, this phantom of Abraham, been laughing at him all along? Was he being punished for the wilfulness of his father's father? Or for the feeble spirit of his father? Or for some inherent flaw that depleted the children of Abraham from generation to generation? Was there even – had there ever been – such a Lord, except in Abraham, Isaac and now Jacob's wishful imagination?

When that first child arrived, the child that Leah called Reuben, it took some time before Jacob could bring himself to look at it. In any case, Rachel kept him beside her for days and nights on end, hardly letting go of his hand, digging her fingernails painfully into his wrist as she wept and writhed with anguish at the humiliation of her sister's fertility and her own childlessness.

'But I love you, only you. Wait; children will come. And anyway, only our love matters now,' Jacob had pleaded.

She was not to be comforted. The sound of the baby crying, carried from Leah's quarters on the wind, convulsed Rachel with envy and loss.

'It doesn't matter. I love you.'

She barely glanced at him, but waved a hand feebly in front of her, batting away the troublesome fly of his consolation.

'It matters. Having children matters. What else could possibly matter?'

'Love. Love matters. Even if you don't have children – but you will, I'm sure you will – my love for you will never lessen.'

She turned her mouth down in disgust, but held tightly on to his hand.

'Don't go to her. Don't go to it.'

'It's all right, my love, she means nothing to me.'

'And the child?'

'Nor the child. Only the child born of our love will count.'

She had some comfort in knowing that Jacob, of all people, could not stand on the ceremony of primogeniture. Yet it was simple truth: Leah had given birth to the firstborn. And she, so loved, so passionately attended by Jacob, had not conceived.

One night, when Rachel slept, Jacob crept out of bed and went to the room where the baby, Reuben, slept with his nurse. Jacob held up a tallow candle and looked at the infant in the dancing shadows. Here was the beginning of Jacob's own household. Whatever his feelings for Rachel, that was, in truth, inescapable. Children were needed if Jacob was to build a world of his own, as his grandfather, and even his father had done. He wanted Rachel's children more than anything in the world – though not more than he wanted Rachel herself – but he had to have children. He could not resist looking at the only life he had made. Reuben appeared to be a healthy enough child; he lay sleeping in his cot, breathing fast, looking pink – what did Jacob know about infants? – but suddenly he sensed how tenuous life was, and saw, as it were, in the warm glow of the candle, the thin skein that held Reuben (and Jacob's future) safe in the world. If he felt anything stirring in him at the sight of the baby, beyond thoughts of posterity, he suppressed it. But he knew that a man had to secure his future – his place in the world after he had gone – as well as his worldly love.

By the time Reuben was weaned, Rachel had still not fallen pregnant. Each month Jacob suffered an agony of noisy misery as Rachel bewailed the bloody evidence of her childlessness before she left for and after she returned from the women's place. He *said* he loved her, but he couldn't, not enough, not properly, or why had she not conceived? If that camel-faced sister of hers had, after a single night with him . . . Jacob sat with his shoulders sagging helplessly. Love had nothing to do with it. Of course, he loved her, like no woman had ever been loved, but there were some women who had difficulty, he had heard. And look at his grandmother, Sarah. She had been an old woman when she got pregnant with Isaac. And his own mother had to wait a long time before she conceived.

'Yes, your family. It's your fault. A rotten line.'

'Give it time. Sometimes these things happen late.'

'Why me? They didn't happen late for Leah.'

'Everyone is different.'

'I don't want to be different,' Rachel screamed. 'I want a child now, not when I'm a hag. I want a child before Leah. I'll never have that, not if I wait for ever.'

Jacob pacified her with caresses, with more lovemaking, stuffing her with children, if only he could, or she could. Their love became desperate; a passion with an end in view is like a stream running into the desert sand. It loses itself. Rachel demanded love in a tone of voice so determined that it made Jacob shrivel. He loved her still, and desired her, but the love they did increasingly came to seem similar in intent to the breeding strategies he tried to work out in the fields with the sheep.

'Oh, my Rachel,' he would murmur, moving towards her.

'Not now,' she'd snap, batting him away from her bed. 'It wouldn't be any good now.'

'What?'

'The older women said. There are better times than others. Not now.'

'But I want, I love . . .'

'There's no point. Leave me alone.'

Jacob put this down to Rachel's engulfing need to have a child, he never thought to doubt her love – fundamental, though subsumed temporarily by the other need – for him. *His* love never wavered, though his mind and body tired. Even so, knowing what he knew about the past of his family, he was compelled to secure the future. Whatever the price he had to pay with Rachel – the tears, the rage, the rejection he would suffer – he had a responsibility to the inheritance he had worked and cheated so hard to achieve.

The weeks after Jacob spent part of a night with Leah in her apartments were long and terrible. Rachel's wrath was very great. She attacked him physically and in every other way she could find. He suffered her blows and her accusations, knowing them to be justified. It was a kind of betrayal (though if only Rachel would see, not a *serious* one), and yet what else could he do? When Rachel conceived, her children would have every kind of precedence and all the love that did not already belong to their mother, but his assurances were no consolation to his beloved, who remained childless as Leah once again began to swell up, and smile that smile of hers.

Simeon, then Levi, then Judah. Each the product of a single coupling after the previous child was sent out to nurse. Each an acknowledgement that Rachel had still not conceived. Four sons; four nights – partial nights – of love, though he did not call it that, with Jacob for Leah. Only the very first actually a night and actually love. Love mistaken. Each time, each of the three times, after that, she opened her arms to him to reiterate the pleasure, the passion and the tenderness they had shared that wedding night of theirs. But Jacob would have none of it. He entered her without preliminaries, without even speaking her name, moved with a grim-faced efficacy towards his climax and, as soon as it was possible, released his future into her. He pushed away her caresses, her mouth, her hands, her words. They touched only at their hips. His eyes did not rest on her body, did not linger on her face. While he penetrated her he kept his eyes wide open, but averted. Each time he arrived in the dead of night and lit all the lamps, so that they enacted their child-making in a midnight blaze of light. There was no end to Jacob's cruelty. No end to his punishment of the woman who had successfully impersonated his love. Through trickery, only through trickery, his eyes told her. Her eyes said what other way was there in this world?

And each time she began to swell and fill out. People remarked the first time about how she had changed, but after that understood that it was a sign of another child coming along. Simeon came, and she wept salt tears on his newborn head, consoling herself and her son for their absent husband and father. 'I have been given you, too, my second son. Be my guarantee of Jacob, my love's future.' Levi came and this time she felt strong and certain again. 'Now, my beautiful boy, my husband will realise who his real wife is, who the mother of his children is. I have secured his dynasty with three sons. Now he will join me.' Judah came, the fourth son, and Leah sobbed over his trembling body. 'My son,' she whispered, pressing her face against his soft sweet skin, and made no mention of Jacob or her hopes.

146

Jacob did not come again. With four sons his line was safe. Life was tenuous, children were frail, but four was enough. He did not come to see the children, though he ensured their welfare. Leah had the status within the household that was due the mother of Jacob's children, but everyone knew she was the childbearing female, not the beloved. In public as in private, Rachel held sway as the true wife of Jacob, noisily and grandly. She ignored the children, averting her eyes from her four nephews.

'Tell that woman to keep her brats out of the way when I leave my quarters,' she screamed at Jacob.

She did not greet her sister when she saw her, as could not be avoided sometimes, but it was evident to Leah that Rachel dare not let her gaze rest on her sister for fear of seeing what burned in her eyes – weak eyes, but now with a capacity to arrest those on whom she turned them. Eyes that held the gaze of others with a discomforting glare of pain and triumph. Eyes that had seen four sons born. Rachel would never have dared risk a direct look into those pale, staring orbs. Weak eyes, they said when she was a child. They were not so weak any longer. Even so, they could not catch the eye of her beloved Jacob. He passed her like a stranger. Ignored her when they were obliged to eat as a family. Even Laban, her father, seeing the way his fortune was now linked with Jacob's work and skills, developed a casual disdain for his oldest daughter. Her eyes had become expressive, but only her children cared to engage with them.

So, a sorry tale of human dissatisfaction. Of things not working out quite the way . . . of things working out with such perversity that one could hardly credit it possible without a scheming, playful, vengeful God somewhere at the back of it. Or a malicious editor. But God had been rejected in favour of human will – the children of Abraham and the God of Abraham had gone their separate ways, it seemed – while editors had not yet invented themselves. Life, these people had concluded from the ensuing silence, was in their own hands, or at any rate in the hands of happenstance. Action or fortune. Good luck; bad luck. With good luck, after all, as likely as the other kind. How simple, how delightful if things fell out the way that was best for everyone. Why shouldn't Jacob have realised that Leah in the dark was Leah in the light? Why should he have loved Rachel so instantly, so purely physically, so irrationally, that even Leah's passionate responsiveness and the gift of children had no effect on his desire? Why shouldn't Rachel's narcissism and limited affection towards her husband diminish his blind passion? Senseless. Or nothing but senses. Common as they come. In any case, in the long run, and the long run was what counted, what did it matter? One woman had the children, the other had the love. The man might feel he was having a difficult time, but wasn't he getting what he wanted? Not all in the same place, but what he wanted; some here, some there? And the women? Getting what they wanted? More or less. Everything more or less. Love or children? To love or be loved? Which would you prefer? Well, you can't have both. Be realistic. Think about the main thing: the dynasty secure, life can go on, generation after generation, the story continues, and that is what matters – what matters in the overall scheme of things, in the long run of the complete narrative. The long run, as any editor will tell you, is the thing. The crucial thing. If the story is to roll on, leave the present actors behind each in their own segment of the tale and continue with a narrative that makes sense – in the long run.

*

'I might as well be dead!' the woman screamed. 'What is the point of my life?'

Sometimes it was hard for Jacob to hold on to the vision he had had of the bright girl walking beside her flock towards the well. But it was the same woman, always loved, always beautiful, always having what she wanted and always unable to tolerate anything less.

'Give me sons! If you don't give me sons, I'm as good as dead. Give me sons, give me sons or I will end it. I warn you, I'll die!'

To the astonishment of both of them, Jacob snapped. For the first and last time he shouted back at her, equalling the force of her scream with a bellow of his own.

'I am not God! I have loved you in every way I could. I've done all a man can do. But I can't make you fertile. It's not in my power. There's nothing I can do about it.'

Immediately there were tears of regret streaming down his cheeks, while Rachel's face, already white and distorted with anger, now froze rigid at the sound of his raised voice. He had never shouted at her before.

'I'm sorry . . . I'm sorry . . .' he wept, reaching an arm out to her. 'I love you, I would do anything . . . but I can't . . .'

And beneath his helplessness there lay a question which teetered on the edge of despair. It was, 'Am I not enough for you . . . Do you not then love me?' It remained unspoken for fear of what Rachel's answer might be. Did she really believe her life with him was meaningless unless she had children? The children were one thing – something that Leah could take care of – but love, what of love? Was that not enough, had it ever been enough for Rachel? Had he simply not noticed that it hadn't been the same for her as for him? Was it possible not to see during all those years that someone did not love you as you loved them? She demanded sons – not just one. Was her passion for equalling her sister greater than her love for him? Was her desire for the honours of matriarchy more powerful than her desire for Jacob? He could not bring himself to ask, to risk an answer that might result, not just in the complication he had previously suffered with Leah's trick, but in the collapse of the emotional centre of his life as if it had never been true, as if he had been merely deluded about Rachel, just as Leah had been deluded about him.

Rachel did not speak. She heard Jacob's unuttered question and considered her future if she were – in her rage – to give the terrible answer and yet still have no children to replace the love she would lose. Fury might have made her respond incautiously, but she held back, enough in control of herself not to risk the loss of everything she had. Being loved, if there were no children, was all she could hope for.

Jacob hung his head in the silence, ashamed and frightened at the reverberations of his raised voice and lack of patience. What kind of love was his that could not understand her needs? Rachel did not take his offered hand. She shut her eyes for a moment and composed herself.

'Well,' she said, seeming to have put her despair behind her, her voice calm and organising; efficient now, resolving her apparently insupportable lack with a solution of her own. 'Then you must sleep with Bilhah, my servant. Take her as your concubine, so that she will give birth and hand the baby immediately to me so that it shall be mine in law. I'll take my place in the dynasty through her.'

So Jacob, a feather in the wind, took a mistress at his wife's command. Bilhah was young and beautiful; she made love lightly, delicately, laughing brightly all the while. His nights with Bilhah were a delight, or they would have been if the thought of his beloved Rachel had not always come between him and the thoughtless pleasure he might have taken. Rachel told him when to go to Bilhah, when the time was most appropriate, and after he returned questioned him about his performance. He could see that something sour now lived at the corners of her mouth, something calculating in the intense blue of her eyes (was it new, had it always been there, surely not?), yet nothing wore the edge off Jacob's love for her.

Bilhah conceived. She gave birth to a son which was laid on the waiting lap of Rachel before its cord had been cut.

'Now I have something to show my sister,' she said, looking down on the child before signalling for it to be taken off her knees. She named him Dan. Then another child by the concubine, and Rachel called him Naphtali. 'Now I am a woman with two sons,' she declared fiercely to the household, parading around the compound with them in her arms before returning them to their nurse and birth mother.

And a storm of belligerence exploded into the life that Jacob was so carefully trying to keep temperate. Open warfare broke out between Rachel and Leah, waged through the lightning conductor of the man they loved. Jacob had not been near Leah since the birth of Judah. Now she demanded that he take her servant, Zilpah, as his concubine too. It was only right, only fair. If he did not, she would dispute the legitimacy of the so-called sons of Rachel, Dan and Naphtali *ben Bilhah* – as she called them scornfully. She would publicly deny that the tradition of adoption held any meaning when he had four truly legitimate sons. Even if her argument was not accepted, it would cause embarrassment and difficulty. If this was a numbers game and

Jacob refused to have any doings with Leah, she would play the game for all it was worth. If the love of Jacob was utterly lost, beating her sister was worth everything. Take Zilpah, she instructed Jacob, make children with her for Leah to adopt, or he would have no peace. Peace was what Jacob wanted. He suffered Rachel's noisy rage at the new turn of events; to be the lover of *her* servant was one thing, but to take Leah's girl to his bed . . . However, she eventually saw the sense in not letting Leah make a public scandal. Zilpah was also young and lovely. Both concubines gave Jacob more pleasure and less trouble than either of his wives, but to Jacob it was beside the point. All he longed for was the contentment of his beloved Rachel, to gain her love and a quiet life.

Zilpah gave birth to Gad and then to a second son, Asher. Leah received them both on her lap and named them as they were pushed into the world by forces beyond their control.

'How fortunate I am,' she announced in a brittle, brassy voice that could be heard throughout the compound. 'How women must envy me. Now I have six sons. Six. Was any woman ever luckier?'

Leah's boys had grown up knowing of their mother's suffering. How could they have avoided it? She raised them to understand that they were the children of a man whom she loved wholeheartedly, but who failed to love her. She had no husband to speak of, but she had sons on whose shoulders she might weep. The years passed and they grew into youths who experienced for themselves how distant their father was to them. Jacob-the-dream may have been deeply loved by Leah, but Jacob-the-man fell far short of what his first wife and her sons wanted from their husband and father. The boys watched him from a distance. When he spoke, it was in tone and matter no different to the way he spoke to his servants, terse instructions, a brief dutiful check to see that everything was all right enough not to need his attention. He needed his attention for his breeding programme with the flocks, and for engaging with his discontented but beloved Rachel. He had not touched Leah for a long time now. Rachel vetoed it, but in any case he had no desire to be with Leah. He had his legitimate sons, and now he had his adoptive sons by Rachel. Yet Leah burned for him, a corner of her dulled spirit still capable of imagining Jacob coming to her at last with a new look of love in his eyes. She was fierce with pride at her sons, the boys she had brought into existence, strong, capable young men who ensured the posterity of the family of Abraham and his grandson Jacob. But still her eyes were pouched and red-rimmed in the morning from weeping. The boys saw her misery and felt the responsibility and helplessness that the children of a loved but not loving father and husband are inclined to feel.

One day Reuben came home from his day's work with a bulging sack which he placed on his mother's knees.

'I found these growing in the field,' he said shyly, opening the sack. 'They're for you.'

She peered down at the several objects he had spilled into her lap. Her eyes were too dim now to make them out even at that small distance. She picked one up and brought it close to her face. The foetid smell that hit her nostrils made her flinch. A stench of something fleshy rotting. It was a plant: root and leaves. The soiled brown root was fat and rounded at the top, then forked, dividing into two thick branches, each narrowing down slowly to pointed ends that had several wispy rootlets coming off them. Two large dark-green oval leaves, wilting now from their time enclosed in the sack, grew straight off the bulbous top of the root, at opposite sides from each other. It presented to Leah's poor vision a crude puppet figure, headless, with arms and legs splayed. Leah dropped it into her lap with the other two plants and smiled up at her son.

'Mandrake,' Reuben said. 'There they were just growing in the middle of the field. They say they scream when you pull them up, but I didn't hear anything. I thought they might . . . help.'

Reuben was Leah's firstborn, a quiet brooding boy, short and dark, with evasive eyes that flicked away from any gaze that caught his furtive glances. He was the son his mother found most moving; a self-elected protector of small helpless creatures, including his brothers when they were little, but with a fearfulness about him as he encountered the world, or rather, avoided it by keeping his eyes carefully lowered when going about his business. He felt things, Leah knew, but spoke very little. He behaved well, always well, intervening when his younger brothers argued, taking his firstborn status seriously, telling them they must not cause their mother to fret. He worried about her, he wanted to make things better for her. His aim was to smooth his mother's sorrow, but he could not. He watched his father striding busily around the place, looking then looking away, both of them receiving his gruff greeting, given only when it was unavoidable, like a physical punishment. He felt Jacob's neglect of him exactly as he felt his dismissal of his mother; it was his, Reuben's, fault somehow, and he had no idea how to improve the situation.

'You're a good boy. The best of all my boys,' Leah said. 'Fancy you knowing about mandrakes. And bringing them to me.' She pulled him down towards her and kissed him on top of

154

his head. 'My precious son. Now put them back in the sack before we choke on their stink.'

'Do you think they will work? That my father will . . .'

'We'll prepare the infusion tomorrow.'

'But how will you get him to take it? He's never here.'

'I'll summon him. I'll demand to see him and he will drink wine with me. He'll do that at least,' she said, but there was uncertainty in her voice.

Reuben wasn't even sure his father would come to see what his mother wanted. The terrible load of her sadness had sat on his shoulders his whole life, and bore down on him now as ever. There was nothing he could do. Perhaps he had been wrong to bring her the mandrakes.

Leah had similar doubts, but then brightened, an old strength returning.

'My son, let's ensure the efficacy of the mandrakes. Magic is good, but it's as well to give it a hand. Spread the word about finding the mandrakes, make sure it is known that you have given them to me. Be overheard telling your brothers about it, overheard by someone who will carry the news to Rachel.'

The canniness of his mother always surprised Reuben. He admired the way she tried to take matters into her own hands. She may have lost the love of her life through her attempt to manipulate him – yes, she told her version of the story to her favourite boy – but it was clear to Reuben, enough of a man to guess at the power of love and the lack of it, that she would not have had it anyway (not that he would ever have said so to his mother). And yet she had tried. She had tried to make what she wanted happen. It hadn't, but wasn't it better to take steps and lose than be helplessly deprived without any effort? It was a question that troubled Reuben. The answer was that the results were the same, yet surely, his young man's pulse insisted, to act was better than to do nothing? And Reuben was heartened once again, when he had grasped what was in Leah's mind, that having brought his mother a little magic for her lost cause, she found the energy and cunning to make it work by not relying on the magic at all.

Rachel arrived at Leah's rooms the next day.

'My dear sister, what a long time since you have honoured me with a visit. Sit, have some tea. Will you eat something?'

Rachel was plumper these days. Being well loved they say can do that. Her lush curves had rounded out even more and stretched the skin, making her look like a ripe pomegranate seed, translucent and bursting with juice. There was even something liquid about her movements, as if her flesh flowed along with her when she moved, like a waterfall concealing the structure of the rocks behind it. Though she was no longer a light-footed girl, she commanded attention, with her straight back and high-held head. Her eyes remained bold and compelling, changing according to the light or perhaps her mood, from bright cerulean to a dusky lilac. Her hair was showing silvery lights among the deep red brown and she wore the mass of it piled up and pinned like an unruly crown, tendrils falling to her neck and down her back. All the delicacy was lost, but she was richer and grander in her beauty now. She paused in the doorway to allow her sister to observe her. As if Leah hadn't always observed her. As if she wasn't instantaneously aware, just like every day of her life, of the differences between them. Leah had, in spite of her childbearing years, become more angular. Her long face was no longer firm in its outline, her jawline was less emphatic and her features seemed in repose to

156

drag at the corners, the edges of her mouth and eyes sloping downwards, deep rills on either side of her nose emphasising the impression of a face falling down and away from its skeleton. When she turned her head, sinewy ropes appeared in her long, scrawny neck. Her robe lay flat against her empty breasts and hung down loosely to her sandalled bony feet. Rachel would be a fat woman in her old age, Leah would wizen. Leah marvelled again that they should be sisters.

There was no remembered warmth in either sister's eyes as they examined each other directly, only recollected history. Usually Rachel swanned past Leah, or sat next to Jacob at family meals laughing and chattering, while Leah sat near the far end of the table with her father, who was always more preoccupied with business talk or whichever concubine was his favourite. Leah had her boys, of course, they remained beside her, and whatever airs Rachel might put on, she could never really conceal her sharp glances at these sturdily growing young men, nor could her public pampering of Dan and Naphtali convince anyone, let alone herself, that they were truly the sons she longed to bear. Now the two women gazed coldly on each other, each to the other the thief of love.

'He desires me as much as ever, you know,' Rachel declared. 'He would be with me every night if I let him.'

'And I have the children.'

Neither accomplishment satisfied either woman, but it gave each the power of pain over her sister. That was something in a life gone awry.

'You have mandrakes,' Rachel said, coming to the point after the stalemate.

'Yes, I have mandrakes. My son, my firstborn, brought them to me.'

Rachel nodded, accepting that defeat.

'Sit, if you like,' Leah said.

Rachel remained standing, and breathed slow and deep for a moment.

'Please give me the mandrakes your son brought you.'

'They say that an infusion of mandrake root cures melancholy. And also that it ensures a restful night's sleep. *Do* sit.'

Rachel dropped heavily onto a pile of cushions and stared down at her hands clutching each other so hard that the pressure turned her nails white.

'I want a child of my own.' The words fighting their way through her clenched teeth, and her eyes fixed on her grasping fingers. 'That's what I need them for. Let me have the mandrakes.'

'Isn't it enough that you have taken my husband from me? Now you want the mandrakes given to me by my son?'

Leah's voice was pitched high. She stood with her back to her sister, the ropes in her neck bulging with the tension of being in control.

'Then let me have the mandrakes – the mandrakes your son brought for you – in return for Jacob spending tonight with you.'

'An exchange of goods? Yes, it's natural for sisters to share. But my mandrakes are worth more to you than one night with Jacob. In return for my mandrakes I will have him once a year, or as soon as I have weaned the child I get from him. That will be the arrangement.'

Rachel shot a look of hatred at her sister, then nodded briefly.

Leah went to the sack on the table and took out the mandrake plants.

'Here,' she said, tipping them into her sister's lap.

Rachel took one, squirming back from the smell and holding it at arm's length, her face a picture of disgust.

'They're filthy.'

'Just earthy. It's what you wanted, isn't it? Take them and go.'

'But give me something to carry them in. I don't want to walk around in the open carrying these for everyone to see.'

'I'm sorry, Rachel, I need the sack my son brought them in. Don't worry, everyone knows how badly you want to conceive. No one will be surprised to see you with my mandrake roots. Just tell them I gave them to you, if they ask. They know I don't need them.'

Not one particle of Leah felt the need to be gracious in this longed-for moment of triumph. Her pains were uncorked and flowed smooth and freely like fine oil towards her sister in distress.

Leah went out to meet Jacob at sunset as he was returning from the fields.

'You are bedding with me this evening. I hired you for tonight and again whenever our next child is weaning, in exchange for the mandrakes my son brought me.'

Her voice was sharp as knives, her mouth twisted with disgust at the tragedy of her life that had turned her husband and her love into a body bought for the night. Her contempt for him was second only to her contempt for herself. Only the pain that her sister was being caused gave her pleasure in this moment. If indeed Rachel was being caused any pain.

She doesn't love you, she never did, she wanted to tell Jacob. Please see it. She is a beautiful, spoiled woman who wants the things she thinks belong to her by right. That is the possession of you and your children. It's not love. I have your children, yet

I only dream of you. I have slept alone all these years, quivering with longing, with the memory of what our bodies were once capable of. I have put up with loneliness of the flesh and loneliness of the spirit, only because I always had a small hope that you would see how wrong you had been. I never thought it was too late. Such a love as ours cannot be too late, cannot run out of time. Now, tonight, we have the chance to make it real again.

But she said none of this. And her hope was buried deep beneath her humiliation at having to order her husband to spend a night with her, and the knowledge that he would do it because it had been sanctioned – demanded even – by the woman he really loved. He looked at her and walked past her towards Rachel's quarters. Later that night he arrived at Leah's bedroom.

'I am here.'

The voice was that of a cold stranger but he was compliant. Leah was almost disappointed. She feared briefly for the sturdiness of her love as her contempt for Jacob's craven acquiescence overwhelmed her for a moment. Was it love or a desire for a quiet life with Rachel that made him do everything he was told? Leah was not sure which motive she despised most in this man whom she had loved to distraction and with desperation all her adult life, and most of her childhood.

He took off his clothes and got into Leah's bed in silence and then began, without touching Leah, to work efficiently at himself, making no attempt to conceal his efforts at self-arousal from the woman lying beside him. She laid a hand on his thigh.

'Jacob,' she tried.

He flinched.

'We have to do this thing. But you will have no more of me than my seed.'

160

He knew how precious he was to her. Earlier that evening, in near-despair, he had questioned how precious he was to Rachel. When he was ready he climbed on top of her and instantly impregnated her. Immediately, he withdrew and made to get up.

'What are you doing?' Leah asked.

'You've had what you paid for. I'm going back to my own bed.'

Leah gasped and then sat up. She found a note of cold determination to put into her voice.

'No. I paid for a night with you. A night was what I bought. A night is what I shall have.'

Without a word, Jacob lay back on the bed, turning on his side, away from Leah. Within seconds he was deeply and unmistakably asleep.

Leah had her beloved for a night. She did not sleep, but caressed and kissed the hours away on his unresponsive body until daybreak came. She noted how he had changed over the years, how age and time had worked on him, enlarging his belly, loosening somewhat the flesh of his inner thighs, roughening further his working hands, swelling the joints of the fingers that she remembered so well from their single dark night so long ago. He snored as he slept. He had not snored that other night they had had together, the night they were married. She whispered her love into his sleep-closed ears, she told him the truth about his life, about the nature of the woman, the other woman, he had married, she told him about her loneliness and about her desire. She took his limp hand and ran it over her body, showing him how she too had changed but that she could nonetheless take all the old pleasure in his touch. He did not stir. Did not skip a breath. He seemed to be more unconscious than asleep. She wept and kept up her loving of Jacob's vacated body. And as soon as dawn broke and the light began so faintly to brighten the window that Leah herself, awake though she was, had not noticed it, he woke, completely and instantly, flung back the quilt that covered him against the night cold, jumped from the bed, dressed and left the room without a glance behind him or a word.

Leah had had her night with Jacob, and his seed, as ever, had taken. Nine months later, she gave birth, in tears, to a fifth son, whom she called Issachar.

'My wages: my son,' she whispered, welcoming him to the world.

She did not forget the arrangement. Barely a year after Issachar was weaned, she gave birth to Zebulun.

'The gifts continue to flow,' she declared to the newborn infant. 'This time, now that I have borne him six sons, my husband will surely honour me.'

Zebulun, barely arrived in the world, could not hear the note, something harsh between a laugh and a shriek, that disturbed his mother's voice. Nor could he notice that the prospect of love had now been drained out of the dregs of her hope. Reuben, keeping watch over mother and infant, did notice. But what could he do?

When Zebulun was weaned, she called Jacob to her again. Nine months later she gave birth. Leah called the child Dinah.

In that same month, Rachel's longings were finally answered and she bore a son at last. It had taken some time for the mandrakes to do their work, but who knows how long magic or desperation needs to be effective?

She called her firstborn son Joseph.

'Finally, the God of my husband has taken away my shame

of being a childless woman. Now may the Lord give me another son.'

Mandrakes, the God of the Hebrews, physical love; it didn't matter to Rachel who or what was responsible for the completion of her life, for her rights at last having been granted. She was happy to thank or praise anything. But dynastically satisfying and physically strong though the baby Joseph was, she knew her triumph must be consolidated with a second son. Even two sons did not absolutely guarantee her position as the next matriarch, after Sarah and Rebekah, of the children of Abraham, but it would be better than the single child that meant she was still vulnerable to the vagaries of fortune – or whatever it might be. Another child would provide a fall-back that would ensure her of the continued existence in the world she so desperately wanted.

'Now,' she said to Jacob. 'You have your firstborn son. I will not feed him myself so that we can make another as soon as possible.'

Jacob did not question aloud Rachel's designation of Joseph as his firstborn. Of course, the birthright belonged to Reuben; Jacob could not risk the chaos that would result in denying the true firstborn his rights and blessing. It was not only his wives from whom Jacob desired a quiet life. The Lord had not been much in evidence since his exile and wandering in the desert, but now Rachel had borne a son. Perhaps the Lord had a hand in it. In any case, it would be as well to keep to the rules when the time came. Jacob knew the cost of breaking them. His love, however, was not committed to the firstborn. Love was not a right. That now belonged, shared with his adored mother, to Joseph, the child Jacob had longed for – Rachel's child. Now, at last, he felt assured of her love.

He was smitten by the baby. The first baby of his that he had been allowed to come close to, the first he had allowed himself to love. He held the child, Rachel's child, and in it belonged all the love he had poured out all these years into Rachel. Finally, he could see the result of love, and Joseph, a fine, alert baby, who gazed up at Jacob and babbled contentedly, was the apple of his father's eye. This was his boy. Joseph was precious enough to Jacob for him not to feel the need for another child by Rachel. How far could one man's love stretch? And knowing that the dynasty did not depend on his youngest son (though he did not say so to Rachel), the urgency for another child was not great. After all, there were eleven sons and a daughter now. However, his desire for Rachel, all these years on, had not at all diminished, and if she now felt the urgent need to have him in her bed again – he had been banished during the whole of her pregnancy – he was not going to refuse himself. Nor was he going to complain at her withdrawal of post-weaning privileges from her sister. Rachel wanted another child, but not at any cost, at least not at the cost of giving the slightest satisfaction to her sister for a moment longer than necessary.

'The debt is paid,' she told Leah, cradling Joseph in her arms. 'Your childbearing days are over.'

So life improved for Jacob. His days of submission between the tempestuous desires of his two wives seemed to have passed. He felt a half-remembered strength of purpose flow back into him After the birth of Joseph, he went to Laban.

'Uncle, it's time for me to go home, back to my place, to my own land. I've served you well in return for my wives and their children. Now, I want to take them home. I have improved your fortunes, now I want to concentrate on mine.'

Laban slowly wagged his head from side to side, appraisingly.

'And what do you want as severance pay?'

'You know how well you've done since I began working for you. Look at the livestock, how healthy, how many they are. You've been richly blessed because of my efforts. Now it's time to consider what I am owed so that I can provide for my own household independently.'

'So,' Laban snapped. 'How much do you want?'

'No money. Nothing that will deplete your wealth.' Laban's eyes widened a little at the improbability and attractiveness of this notion. 'I won't leave immediately. I'll go back to looking after your flocks, but today I'll remove all the dark-coated sheep and the speckled and spotted goats. They can be your gift to me for the work I've done for you. When I leave, I take those sheep and goats and their offspring with me.'

Laban did some calculating. Jacob wanted the spots. Well, he could have them. There were hardly more than a handful in each of the flocks. Perhaps he was slow-witted after all, perhaps the increase in his livestock was not due to Jacob's management. Whatever the cause – good fortune or skill – Laban had indeed been enriched, during Jacob's long stay, with sheep and goats by the multitude, and nearly all of them blossom white if they were sheep and evenly black if they were goats.

'That will be fine,' he said casually. 'It's a deal. You shall have what you ask, my boy. When will you be leaving?'

'Not for a while, Uncle. We'll let a few breeding seasons pass so that I can train my successors and make sure the handover goes smoothly. You can rely on me.'

Jacob had indeed learned a lot about animal husbandry, as well as the human kind, over the years working for his uncle.

After Laban had taken his pure white and pure black animals far enough away from Jacob's parti-coloured herd so that there was no chance of them interbreeding, Jacob put the learning he had acquired during his years in the fields to good use. He only allowed the most vigorous animals to breed together, the weaker ones he put to one side and let them breed with each other – these latter mostly produced less robust uni-coloured offspring which by agreement were Laban's. The stronger animals gave birth to a higher proportion of parti-coloured goats and dark sheep which were sturdy and good breeders in the next season. But Jacob had learned the lesson of his family well. It was not enough to apply knowledge, to *do* in the world; it was as well to employ *belief*. What harm could it do? Indeed it disguised cunning with folk magic and made a knowing herdsman lucky or blessed or something altogether beyond the power of an angry uncle. He concealed his breeding programme with ancient superstitions: let the goats look at stippled twigs, and the sheep look at the brindled goats when they were in heat, and it was common knowledge that they would give birth to a version of what was before their eyes. Trickery, yes, but at least not obviously out-and-out learned skill which can so much more aggravate people. Trickery, yes, but at least being seen to put faith in faith, in case the Lord should be in fact keeping watch over the grandson of the man who once challenged his God and caused love and silence to ensue. Jacob was a son of his fathers – even of the father who appeared to make no moves himself in the world, but who had, after all, allowed his younger son to steal the birthright he was better fitted to honour from his rightful firstborn. Trickery, yes. Jacob the cunning one, the trickster, had only been dormant. Self-interested necessity had roused him.

Within just a few seasons of breeding and careful buying and selling, Jacob had achieved substantial wealth from his dark-coated sheep and speckled goats. His complement of servants grew, his sons worked in his and their future interest and increased the wealth still further. Rachel dressed even more richly now and wore the signs of her husband's success around her neck, in her ears, and on her fingers. Her son wore soft-woven, fine-dyed fabrics such as his brothers had never had. Even Leah, in her own sphere, the mother of the tribe of Jacob's children, a satellite matriarch, walked about with a new layer of self-possession. The whole household developed a look of substance and independence. It became itself: the House of Jacob. And the sons of Laban began to notice their cousin's air of well-being; his many flocks of sheep and goats – all undeniably his by their colouring, and the camels and donkeys he had acquired by judicious trading, the accoutrements of wealth. They went to their father, fearful that if this continued they would lose their own inheritance to their burgeoning relative.

'He tricked you,' they shouted at him.

'How?' Laban shouted back, not disagreeing but unable quite to see how it had happened.

'Is he wealthy? Are his riches close now to ours? Did you intend when you made the deal with him that he should become as substantial as us?'

'No.'

'Then he tricked you. Everything he has comes from you. Those handful of sheep and goats you agreed to let him have – where's our profit on them?'

As Jacob's household expanded, Laban's scowl deepened. Jacob watched carefully. One evening he sent a servant to Rachel and Leah and the children, calling them out to the field where he was overseeing the flocks. They sat in their two separate matriarchal parties of incommensurate size in the dusk and Jacob presided over the conference.

'I had a dream last night. The God of Abraham, my grandfather, came to me and told me to return to the land of my fathers.'

Leah said nothing, but Rachel gasped and jumped up, waving her arms wide to describe the geography of her anxiety.

'To Canaan? Across the desert? Why, when we have so much here? Why would you drag me and our little one through the wilderness to go to some primitive hole we've never seen and that you ran away from? How can you think of it? And to announce it, like this, in public, without consulting with me. Have you gone mad?'

Jacob remained calm; there was a firmness in his voice that Leah recognized from her grim nights of lovelessness with him, and which her older children knew from working under his instruction in the fields. It was new only to Rachel.

'The Lord will be with us, Rachel. In any case, if you don't want to lose your wealth and maybe even your husband, we must move on. Your father hates me. He is angry and jealous of my success. It would be dangerous to stay.'

Rachel gave a little shriek. She dragged Jacob to one side, pulling him by his sleeve to get his private ear, and half-whispered, half-screamed her fury and fear. *She* had not noticed anything amiss. Jacob had told her nothing about this, and now, to be formally instructed, so officially, as if she were just part of the household – it was outrageous. Her father would never do anything to hurt her. He loved her, and if Jacob loved her . . .

'How can you doubt it?' he asked in an undertone. 'But this is something you must trust me about. It is dangerous to stay.

168

Perhaps Laban would not hurt you, but your brothers look at my children with calculating eyes. Think of Joseph. This is a decision I must make and we all must act on immediately.'

'But you should have told me first, in private,' Rachel hissed. 'Not as if I were just one of . . .'

'I couldn't risk telling you before. We must get away quickly. Everyone must move together and no word get back to Laban or your brothers. Please, Rachel, we'll talk about it later, when we're on the move.'

'But Canaan . . .' Rachel moaned. 'Can't you make it up with Father?'

'Your father has cheated me all these years. He paid me a pittance and used me to enrich himself. The deal I made with him was a trick, but only in as much as I had skills he and his sons lacked. All I did was recoup my losses. And I only had the skills and the fortune because the Lord of my forefathers was with me – probably. Now we must go back to the land the Lord promised my family. It's where I belong, and as my wife, it's where you belong too. It's our destiny. A long time ago, when I was alone in the wilderness, I made a promise to build an altar to God in return for his protection. Last night the Lord reminded me of my promise, and said that it was time I went back and kept it. Under the circumstances, it would be the safest thing to do. The God of Abraham can be as dangerous to cross as your father.'

Jacob's wives, polytheists by upbringing and therefore practical in matters of faith, knew it was as well to keep any god happy. Perhaps they feared Jacob's family deity more than he did, believing in him as much as they believed in any deity and more perhaps than Jacob himself. The existence or otherwise of the Lord of Abraham (and therefore his power and danger) was a more critical matter to those who had only him to believe in. Leah and Rachel took the Lord as seriously as they took their own household gods, or any other that might impinge on their lives. Keep them on your side, that was the thing, and with any luck they will let you get on with your life as best you may. An unkept promise to a god was a dangerous thing. Better to go and build the altar than risk the wrath of that Lord as well as Laban and Jacob. And there were other considerations.

'Do you really believe that you or I will get any inheritance from our father,' Leah said to Rachel, pulling her to one side. 'He has used up our dowry in the labour of Jacob on his land. Whatever Jacob (and his Lord) have retrieved from Laban's wealth is only what he owes the two of us, and our children.'

Rachel looked hard at Leah, and then nodded sharply, all the rivalry, haughtiness and fear of removal to primitive places subsumed for the time being beneath a new practical solidarity with her sister.

'Yes, Jacob,' she said, turning to her husband. 'Whatever your Lord has said you should do, we must do.'

3

It wasn't until he was an old man, in mourning for his favourite son, that Jacob realised how all his life he had lived with dread. A knife paring away his insides. A terror scraping at the back of any quiet or contented moment. A looming shape in the mist, a disturbance just outside vision, a feared something that came towards him. Always waiting. Until now, he had not known what it was he feared. The worst. Events, bad things happening: that was as far as Jacob had gone in defining what he dreaded. And when something terrible did occur, each time he thought that finally his fears had come true, the worst had happened. Until the next catastrophe, more insupportable than the last. Loss upon loss. Wound upon wound. First the failure of family, then the disfiguring of love. And it went on. The violated child, the end of his beloved, the contempt of his children. There could be nothing more, surely? Yet this loss, the final depriva-tion – this time there could be nothing worse to come, because the death of his son Joseph encompassed all the other losses, and more besides. But now, with everything gone, he still felt the old corroding anxiety. For what? There was nothing else to lose, nothing worse that could occur. It was a betrayal of his grief still to fear what might be to come. Yet he did.

With no more to lose it might have occurred to him that what he had always feared was not an event, but a truth: his smallness, his incommensurateness with his grandfather, Abraham, who had shouldered the burden of inventing posterity, who was given or invented for himself a purpose out of the nothingness, the blankness, the mere contingency of life. Somewhere between God and the idea of generations, Abraham had found a meaning, had sensed himself large enough to have visions or mould from his seed a future beyond blank non-existence. And what a moment it was for the children of Adam. It was the first great human leap over the chasm of death. A leap of imagination, surely, but all the greater, all the more heroically human for that. The son, Isaac, crippled by Abraham's implacable vision and eclipsed by the size of his father looming above him with his hand raised, trembled and withdrew into pathology and ennui to lead the confined life of a shadow, barely a man, more of an unappeasable appetite unable to discharge itself except in the crudest of physical satisfactions.

Jacob considered the two men, his grandfather and his father, and saw nothing of Abraham in himself. He averted his eyes, refusing to look any longer, for fear of who he would see. For fear that Isaac – the chasm that he had hoped to overleap – was his true inheritance. Jacob, the son of the son, was not certain that his had been anything but an accidental life, and worse than that, an ordinary life. Where there had seemed, in his youth, a point – the wresting of the birthright and blessing from his older twin, the epiphany of love that would lead

172

towards the future indicated by his grandfather, the creation of wealth and standing in the world – there now turned out after all to be none. None of the things he had acted on had provided the fulfilled old age he imagined he had been building. Why had he fought so hard for precedence, held on so tightly to his brother's heel when he had already lost the battle for the first light? No God-of-Jacob had ever appeared to him in a waking vision, offering him a new name and a new world. He had only ever had dreams about the God of Abraham reiterating old promises, which, for all he knew, had themselves been no more than dreams or delusions. When he slept in the desert during his first exile in the wilderness, God had promised to be with him, to see him safely back to his home and destiny. A dream. Where had God been during those leaden years working for Laban, when his hopes of a single great love and future had bifurcated and dispersed? Or later, when all the terrible things began to happen? The losses. And when he got home at last, and thought his life fulfilled enough, and at least settled, ready to be an old man, though a widower, full of years and sur-rounded by the love and respect of his heirs, destiny turned out to be the tearing apart of his greatest treasure, his favourite son, by a wild animal. With Joseph stolen from him, nothing that remained had any value. Finally, there was formlessness and futility. What had once seemed like a trajectory, a continuation of a line, was now shown to have been a phantasm. There was no story, only life and death, disordered, pointless and acciden-tal. And Jacob, the son of the son, not of the grandfather – that self-imagined father of a multitude, more numerous than the stars or grains of sand on the seashore, blessed for his sake, remembered always for that blessing – Jacob, son of Isaac, was, after all, nothing more than ordinary. Quite unremarkable. A small man. Who would remember him beyond his time? Who would give thanks for him in generations to come and thereby confer on him a life after death?

Perhaps he could have come to terms with the loss of an assured destiny. He could have settled for the comforts and contentment of a respected old man surrounded by a loving family, enjoying the fruits of his accumulations. He might have relinquished his grander ambitions if only wealth and reverence had provided a semblance of posterity in the here and now. But even that was no more than a dream. He was to die a disappointed, humiliated and unloved old man with twelve – no, eleven – sons who were, compared to the extraordinary first child of Rachel, compared to his hopes, nothing. Even Benjamin, the youngest, who was now all he had left of Rachel although the cause of her irreparable loss, could not make up for the golden boy, Joseph. Now Benjamin would have to remain a child, protected and cosseted, whose loss was always imminent. He could not be seen to be striding towards the future. Jacob could not dare to let him replace what he had seen in Joseph. With the loss of Joseph, Jacob lost heart. Only Joseph, of all Jacob's achievements, seemed to be a reaching towards something great, a connection back to the grandfather; and now Joseph and all Jacob's hope were consumed, nothing more than a bloody remnant. The sons of Leah and the sons of the concubines, his remaining sons, aside from the child who must be kept forever a child, were just men. Just more small men like himself. The ordinary sons of an ordinary man. Jacob son of Isaac, a man of no particular destiny. And because this truth was finally upon him, he howled and rent his clothes, and called out the name of Joseph without cease because he could not bear the silence in which that truth lurked.

Poor old Jacob had hoped to find his story in his remembering, but, of course, his story was only part of the story, one
among many stories, which, without an editor's touch, an
arranger's eye, looked – even to him in the end – much like
anyone else's story. Destiny had to wait for its editor to take
charge, and then, naturally, it wasn't Jacob's story; it was mine.

Twenty years had elapsed since Jacob crept off alone and
empty-handed into the wilderness and found himself, at sunset,
in a darkness he had never before imagined. Now, as the faint
rays of dawn began just barely to take the edge off the night on
the outskirts of Laban's fields, he gathered his wives and children, his concubines, his servants, his camels, his herds of sheep
and goats, and all the worldly goods that were indisputably his,
and led them into the Negev to start the journey back to Isaac,
his father, in the land of Canaan. The caravan left Haran in
silence, the camel drivers whispering to their charges to keep
them quiet, the women shushing the excited younger children.
Jacob took advantage of Laban's absence at a festival of sheep
shearing three days' journey away. He left under cover of darkness, travelling into the growing light of day with everything he
rightfully possessed.

Rachel took something more. The night before, Rachel crept
into the family chapel and stole the small carved images of her
father's household gods. Where they were, prosperity and well-
being was assured. Whoever possessed them held the authority
of the family. Jacob had his God-of-Abraham, and she paid
her respects to him, but she was not going to leave anything
behind that might limit her fortune. A little extra help would do
no harm. The more gods she owned, the better.

Laban and his men, unhampered by twenty years of worldly

goods, wives and livestock, took only a week to catch up with Jacob's caravan.

'Thief! Betrayer!' he bellowed at his son-in-law. 'You've abducted my daughters and run off like a criminal. You only had to tell me you wanted to go and I'd have seen you off properly with feasting and songs. But you chose to make a fool of me. To creep away. My men are just waiting for the word . . .'

Jacob, remembering another feast, fourteen years before, did not regret missing this last one.

'I'm sorry, Laban,' Jacob said, hanging his head in an effort to appease. 'I was worried that you would try to deprive me of my wives and children if I told you I was going. I can't imagine what I was thinking of. But everything I have taken is mine.'

'That's not true. Not my household gods,' Laban shouted. 'You stole my gods.'

Jacob was startled.

'I've stolen nothing. I'm sorry I left so hurriedly, but I wouldn't take your gods. What reason would I have? I've got a God of my own. I'm telling you the truth. Look around the camp, search everywhere; if you find anything that is yours, take it. If you find your idols in my camp, tell me. I swear to you that whoever stole them will die.'

Laban, after his furious pursuit, found only contrition, good manners and the promise of recompense. He swept out of Jacob's tent and ordered his men to search the camp. He kept the search of close family – Jacob, Leah and Rachel – for himself. Finding nothing in the first two tents, he arrived at Rachel's. She was reclining languidly against some pillows, sitting on the cushioned saddlebags of the camel she rode, and in which she had hidden the icons she stole.

176

'Out you go, I want to search the tent,' Laban ordered, glad to be able to order anyone to do anything.

'I'm sorry, father, I can't.'

'What?'

'Can't.' She raised her shoulders helplessly, a small smile of embarrassment widened her mouth.

'Can't? Can't? There is no *can't* when a father orders his daughter to do something. You will get up right now, and leave the tent. Do you hear me?'

Rachel nodded, and then shook her head.

'Sorry. I can't.'

Laban stared rebellion in the face and wondered what to do about it.

'Rachel, you have to do as I say. Get up, now or there'll be trouble. I'm still your father . . .'

He moved towards her, ready to lift her bodily to her feet. She raised her palms to him. Had the smile of embarrassment turned the corner into triumph?

'No, don't touch me. Father, please, don't be angry, but I can't get up at the moment. Just before you came in I felt my . . . you know . . . coming on . . .'

'What?'

'I'm unwell . . . My woman's trouble . . . I'm bleeding, Father. It would be better if I stayed where I was while you are in the tent. You're welcome to search the tent when I've gone to the women's place, but do be careful not to touch anything where I've been sitting, it's where my period came on. It's as unclean as I am.'

Laban stopped still with his hands frozen in their readiness to pull Rachel from her seat. If he had touched her, or anything she had touched, or, the gods forbid, anything her menstrual blood had touched, he would have been contaminated. His mouth twisted in disgust.

'Ach, women,' he spat. 'Did I come all this way for women and their bleeding?'

'No, you came for your possessions. But nothing in Jacob's camp is your possession any more, Father. Now if you'll be kind enough to excuse me, I need to see to myself.'

Laban hurried out of the tent.

'So,' Jacob demanded, full of ignorant confidence. 'Did you find anything?'

Laban shook his head briefly. Jacob took his moment of triumph and made the most of it, enjoying every rising syllable of complaint against his nonplussed father-in-law.

'So what crime have I committed? What am I guilty of to make you chase after me like this and search through my possessions? I've worked for you for twenty years, and kept your animals safe and well. I've even borne the loss of any that were taken by wild animals or stolen. Day and night, night and day, I've sweated and frozen for you and your wealth. Even when I might have rested I couldn't. I've lost the ability to sleep like a normal person with all the years of waking nights looking after what is yours. And how do you thank me? With accusations and threats of violence. Well, *my* Lord has seen my suffering and he decided last night that enough was enough and that I should take what is rightfully mine and go home.'

Laban silently added Jacob's refusal to offer him a face-saving exit to his list of grievances against his son-in-law. He tried to find one for himself.

'It's *all* mine. Everything you see here is mine. Daughters, grandchildren, sheep, goats. Even the clothes on your back.

Where did you get them, except from me? But what can I do? You've upped and gone. You've taken them from me.' He sighed dramatically. Deeply wronged, a man of peace unwilling to spill blood no matter what injustice had been done to him. 'Well, well, never mind, we'd better make a pact. I'm not one to hold grudges about what's done. But from now on you had better take care of my daughters and grandchildren – good care, mind, my boy. And don't even think of taking any other wives. My fury can be terrible. For now, let's call a peace. You stay on your side of the line and I'll stay on mine.'

Stones were gathered and laid to mark the spot.

'Swear this by your God,' Laban demanded solemnly, almost priest-like now in his pacifism.

'I swear,' Jacob smiled, enjoying Laban's pompous discomfort.

'By your God,' Laban insisted.

'I swear by my God,' Jacob said, and added, suddenly no longer smiling, nor paying much attention to Laban, 'By the Terror of my father, Isaac.'

Laban scrutinised his son-in-law carefully to see if there was a threat in his extraordinary description of his God, but Jacob had now turned his gaze towards the desert, and his eyes, screwed up with the effort of looking into the invisible distance, seemed to be seeing something that was indeed terrible. Laban shrugged, a god sworn on was a god sworn on, whatever you called him, and Jacob's private terrors were not his concern. With his face saved, enough at least for public show, Laban and his party made ready to leave the camp.

'Come,' Jacob announced to his people first thing next morning, when the camp had been packed up. 'We are going home.'

179

No one among the company was quite sure what Jacob meant by that. And, in truth, Jacob was far from sure himself.

Leah, well into middle age, with her six boys and Dinah, Jacob's only daughter, was less sure than anyone about the meaning of the *home* she was going to. She watched her life being packed on to the camels for a journey to who-knew-where. A woman with so many grown sons carries with her an internal security, as well as the practical comfort of their sturdy concern for their mother. But they were going to Canaan, to live among the Hebrew descendants of Abraham. She was a stranger walking towards a strange land, and all the protection in the world, all her pride in her strong children, could not save her from fear of an alien future, nor from the memory of an alien past. She would be in an unknown land with the man she loved, but who did not love her, who only brought her along because her sons would not have stood for her being left behind, and perhaps because Jacob wished to demonstrate to his former employer that for better or worse she was Jacob's wife and not Laban's daughter. She was there as chattel, as a convention (a wife's a wife, however despised), as a slap in the face for her father. But still, Jacob travelled with Rachel and her single, whining, attention-seeking child whose desire to shine equalled only that of his mother's desire for him to shine. The boy answered all questions, whether put to him or not, whether he knew what he was talking about or not; he preened in his fine clothes, and advised anyone who stayed to listen how to improve whatever they were doing. Once Leah had watched young Joseph explain to Reuben the best way to milk the goats. Reuben continued pulling smoothly on the nanny's teats in silence until he couldn't stand it any more. 'And now, little brother, go away. Right now.

Don't start the sentence you are about to speak. Just go. Take an older brother's advice.' The tone in which this was said, quiet, but with an edge of desperation, persuaded the lad that he had finished his discourse on milking. Jacob doted on him, as much as on Rachel. He could still be seen reaching out to touch her cheek, whispering private things into her ear, and shaking his head in wonderment that he should have the good fortune to be the husband of such a woman. She never requited his physical attentions in public, but she did not try to stop them, and the haughtier and more distant she was, the greater was Jacob's look of longing. It was with Rachel that he discussed his plans, and his purposes, not with his first wife. He loved her still, as he still did not love Leah. She knew now that would not change. Wherever they were going would be – there was no longer the possibility of doubt – as loveless for Leah as where they had been for the past twenty years. And stranger.

Jacob, however, to Leah's feeble but astute eyes, clearly had other concerns too. Everyone knew the road to Canaan was not going to be an uneventful trek. Word had come that the tribal lord of Edom was travelling northwards towards them with a retinue of four hundred men. A regiment, or a raiding party. This lord was spoken of with respect, even fear, by wandering nomads, and now he was known to be at Seir on the steppes of Edom, on a direct course for Jacob's caravan. This lord of Edom was especially to be feared by Jacob, his brother: his younger brother by a mere infant's body, his older brother by virtue of deceit, cunning and theft. Esau had learned, as he'd had to, to live well by his sword, and made a life of his own in Edom as a warrior and a hunter. In the two decades that had passed, he had grown from the wild weeping boy who had been tricked out of what was his by birth, into a self-sufficient man of substance who had gathered followers and wealth around him. After the theft of his blessing, he had not pursued Jacob, perhaps out of an initial despair, an inability to do anything at all that had come over him for a time when he realised that the mistake his father had made was not one he regretted. But after the apathy, Esau no longer had the wish to devote himself to revenge. Or rather, he traded the satisfactions of revenge for a worldly position, for a place of his own which eventually he became strong enough, without the assets of birthright, to make *truly* his own.

Leah could see the fear in Jacob's drawn face when he rose and walked about the camp that morning. She remembered the days, brief days, when they were friends and Jacob had confided the truth to her, how he had to flee from the rage of his dangerous brother, the justified rage of a twin who had been tricked by his sibling. She recalled her young friend, her secret love, his face drained of colour and creased with the pain of shame and fear as he spoke about Esau. And now, again, he had that look. Not relief at having thrown off the burden of being Laban's servant, and heading towards his own land again after so long, but deep internal terror at having once again to face his brother, Esau, who was marching with his men steadily north towards them.

When everyone was ready to set off, and the two families, the large and the small, the loved and the unloved, were collected around Jacob, he called for messengers and told them to ride south to meet up in advance with Esau's oncoming party.

'Listen carefully, tell him this, exactly as I say it: This is a message to the Lord Esau from his servant Jacob. I went to Haran to stay with Laban, where I have been ever since we last met. I have accumulated oxen and donkeys and sheep and servants. I am simply a man and his goods in transit. I want you to know that your servant Jacob is heading in your direction, my lord Esau, in the hope that you will meet him on friendly terms.'

Leah and the rest listened to Jacob's ingratiating message, the son with the blessing calling his rough and ready brother *lord*, and only Leah was not surprised. Jacob looked sickly, as if the sun and winds had not daily scorched his skin these twenty years, his voice wavered, barely reaching the women and children who stood around him, and Leah knew that it was not just fear of all he had to lose, but also the shame of having finally to confront one to whom he had done a wrong. He feared not just his brother's wrath, but his brother's face. He dreaded the pain of Esau's knowing eyes on him. He had swept away his past these last years, and now it galloped towards him, as fresh as yesterday, to stare him in the face. He had been in hiding, and now he was to be recognised and confronted face to face. And why, Leah wondered, does he not fear *my* face, why does Jacob not tremble under the gaze of my poor eyes? Does hatred override guilt, and justify cruelty? Wasn't her trickery just the mirror of his own? She had faced him all these years, and borne his hatred. Well, let him fear his brother's eyes. It was right and proper that he should. Let him feel terror for the misery he caused someone else, even if he felt no terror at facing her. She had paid the price for her night of deceit with Jacob by being forever unloved. In the emptiest moment of her life, as she watched the camp being taken apart that morning, Leah hoped fervently that Esau would take his revenge on Jacob, even if it meant the death of all of them.

By the time the messengers returned, they were camped on the north side of a tributary of the Jordan river known as the Jabbok. Esau had listened to Jacob's message but had made no reply. Jacob was shaken at the news.

'He said nothing?'

'Nothing.'

'But he is still heading towards us?'

'Yes. They will be south of the Jabbok by tomorrow.'

Jacob covered his mouth with his hand. After a moment he spoke.

'Divide everything into two camps. Sheep, cattle, camels, goods and people. Two separate groups.'

Leah supposed that he planned to save half of what he had, hoping that Esau's rage would be sated by slaughtering the people and repossessing the goods of just one of the groups. She sensed a desperate determination to cling to the material remains of his life in the face of spiritual annihilation. Leah watched as her beloved contemplated the loss of everything he had salvaged from twenty years of exile, of love gone wrong, of bad faith, of a wish to go home and make his peace with life. He spun round and walked off a little way, muttering to himself.

'Lord of Abraham . . . Lord of Isaac . . . promised . . . all would be . . . my brother . . . save me . . . future . . .'

The waiting assembly heard the gist of his prayers carried back on the wind, spoken in a hissing complaint. In the ensuing silence everyone stood, wondering whether the time had come to scatter, to run back to Laban, to do whatever each thought the best way to remain alive.

Jacob finally returned.

'I will send a gift to my brother, one fitting for such a great and powerful lord. Enough to placate him.'

He ordered that the next day his shepherds and cattlemen were to arrange generous sized herds of goats, sheep, camels, cows and asses, and put each herd in the charge of a group of servants. They were to meet Esau herd by herd, one after another.

'When the first herd arrives, tell Esau that his servant Jacob has sent it and that more is coming. I will meet him when all the gifts have been presented. Send the herds one after another, in a great wave so they seem never to end.'

Leah could not hold her tongue any longer.

'Are you returning part of his birthright? Will it be enough to repay all the years of his anger?' she called out.

Jacob's eyes burned into her as they had not done for many, many years, not since he discovered that it was she and not Rachel he had called out to in love that first night. His look of loathing was no less now than it was then. Leah bore his gaze for a moment before replying to her own question.

'No, I don't think it will be enough.'

At dusk, Jacob crossed the Jabbok ford with his two wives, Leah and Rachel; their two servants, Bilhah and Zilpah; all their children, his servants and his goods. He ordered them to separate into two camps and waited until they had settled.

'I'm going back to the north side of the stream to spend the night alone.'

'You're going to leave us here?' Rachel gasped.

'With the servants. Just for tonight. I need to be alone.'

'And tomorrow? When your brother reaches us?' Rachel's voice had risen to the edge of panic.

'I'll be here tomorrow. Before dawn. Of course.'

Leah wondered. Were they to be part of the tribute Jacob paid his brother for his life, if the earlier procession of gifts failed to appease? Could he be so foolish? It was Jacob that Esau wanted, Leah was certain of that, as certain as a scorned human being could be. There was a stubborn look on Jacob's face that tried to suggest he knew what he was doing. A night alone, alone with his God, he implied, to prepare. Or was it just fear and the need to put a wall of people and a stream between

185

himself and his terror? Rachel was breathing so hard that her servant had to half-carry her to her tent. Love it seemed was letting her down. Not even Jacob's undying love could compete with the terror of having to face his guilt. Or so Leah thought as she watched the love of her life turn away from everything he had come to possess over the past two decades and go back across the Jabbok ford with nothing but a staff in his hand.

It was the first night he had spent entirely alone since he first went into the wilderness to escape the anger of his brother Esau, all those years before. He saw the scathing look in Leah's eyes and the mistrust on Rachel's face when he promised to return the next day. Leah's contempt was to be expected, and he cared nothing for it, but that Rachel should doubt him. How could she think he would leave them to their fate; allow them – Rachel! Joseph! – to become hostages to Esau?

Yet he was not quite certain himself why he had returned to the north side of the Jabbok. To be alone, he had said. For what? To do what? To prepare himself. But what preparation could he make, alone in the dark with nothing and no one around him? Better surely to make a battle plan ready in case Esau attacked them. Or an escape plan. But for either of those he needed to be with his people. To be a leader. What could he do alone to assuage his terror of what tomorrow would bring? Listen for the Lord? The Lord of Abraham, the Terror of Isaac, and – at last? – the Comfort of Jacob? Wait for the Lord to make him his own, to give him his future, his assurance of security. To rename him as he had his grandfather. A change, a renewal, the rebirth of Jacob into someone with the Lord's strength for the coming fight. Hadn't he done enough, the son of the son, for that?

186

But even while he was waiting for the Lord, he knew he would never hear the Lord's voice – outside himself, not dreamed, not imagined, but out there in the world – which he only half-believed that Abraham had heard. He craved the sound of a wide-awake, and therefore reliable assurance that there was something more-than-him watching and minding about the particle of existence that was Jacob. He longed for that voice, for the relief of it, for the ease of it, for the alleviation from the weight of his guilt and uncertainty, for the assurance of worth. *Why won't he speak?* And at the same time: *How can what never existed speak?* And: *What would such a voice be worth?* Still, he craved silence and solitude during this night, as he never had before.

Or was he really, as Leah supposed and Rachel feared, just running away? Suddenly, he was not so completely sure that he would rise in the dawn and cross back to the other side of the stream. What was to stop him, free of encumbrances, proceeding north as the light rose? Not, of course, into Laban's territory – but there were other directions, other places. He had arrived at a strange land with nothing once before and made a life. He could do it again, though he was not so young, and could not hope to meet a Rachel, a love who turned years into days. It wouldn't be the same, but it could be done, and perhaps turning away from everything – everything except his fear – was the renewal, the only renewal he could hope for. Just leave the crushing ache, the responsibility, the wives who loved and perhaps didn't love him, the grown children who, though they worked as part of the family group, remained always concealed in some way from him, their eyes never directly on his, who spoke when spoken to or when they had something businesslike to say, but who, mother's sons and mother's daughter that they were, always carried a shimmer of resentment about with them. Leave it all. Start again, with nothing but a staff and the will to be someone else. Why should he confront his brother? His stupid brother who let his birthright and his blessing slip away for greed – at least the loss of birthright; the blessing he lost because it did not occur to him to distrust his mother and his brother. Stupidity. Everything must be distrusted. Wasn't he, right now, considering abandoning everyone in order to avoid the unknown consequences of meeting someone whom he had wronged? One shouldn't even trust oneself. It had not even crossed his mind when he determined to spend the night alone by the banks of the Jabbok that he might just run away. And yet, here was the thought, as thoroughly considered and justified as if he had been thinking it for days. Fully formed, like a secret plan he had been hatching and keeping from everyone, including himself. He was not even shocked to find himself considering running away.

It would be a kind of remaking of himself. What need did he really have for the Lord of Abraham when he had already remade himself? First he had transformed himself from Jacob into Esau with mere kidskin and stolen clothes. From dreamer to man of action. Then he had become a wanderer in the desert: a penitent. Then a lover: a giver of himself. Then a student of husbandry: a shepherd and a stockman. Then a man of substance, grandly crossing the desert to settle back in his homeland with an entire caravan of people and things, all his own. Why not become someone else? Cross out all that went before and become the new man that he craved the Lord would make him. A self-made new man. Had he after all crossed over the border of the Jabbok stream in order to cross over into a new life? It could be so. He had only to walk in a certain direction to be, yet again, something new. Someone who had left the past behind. The past he had thought he had left behind already.

A kind of fever overcame him at the possibility of a great new betrayal, discarding the expected and rejecting the merely decent. He experienced the thrill of the possibility of dismissing duty and morality from his life, of sloughing off and abandoning the burdens of any kind of guilt. A new wilderness opened up inside him, unlike the old one when he had first set off into the desert to escape the consequences of his behaviour, this time offering him a chance to be free in a way that he had never before imagined. To belong to no one, to owe no one anything, to refuse the slightest commitment to others, to the past. It was, he saw, possible. This night, alone by the banks of the Jabbok, was a turning moment, a place and time where he might cut himself loose from every bond. He shuddered with fear and excitement at the loneliness and the cleanness of such a prospect. Who before him had defied all the rules of life and got away without crawling on his belly punished and begging for forgiveness? Without that voice they called the Lord he was free. He could walk northwards to a life where he renewed his solitude, his terrible freedom, every day, where all the god he needed was his own self, isolated in the vacuum of his mind and heart. He sat with his back resting against a boulder by the side of the stream and listened to the sound of the running water whose gurglings now started to echo and reverberate as if the darkened world were a tent whose walls had suddenly lifted to expose a vast incalculable emptiness. Jacob, mortal and mortally afraid, shivered and gasped at such lack of containment, but like the stream, some part of his spirit surged bright and clean at the desertedness he sensed. Here was the possibility of another

kind of relief from the one he had hoped for from the Lord – or
perhaps the same kind of relief under a different guise.

Jacob was a battle ground, a space where fearsome ghosts –
his grandfather, his father, Esau, his mother, Rachel, Joseph, the
world of connectedness, of intention – reared up and fought for
their meaning against Jacob's emptying, terrified and exalting
soul. He wrestled against the way of the world, the claims and
counterclaims, love, hate, duty, posterity, with nothing but the
perfect blankness of death and futility on his side. He was all
clarity, icy water rushing in a stream, accidental and eternal; but
the ghosts muddied the stream with their insistence on their
own meaning, making the transparent water turbid with deep
explosions of implication. Cobwebby tentacles wrapped around
Jacob, demanding recognition, while Jacob battled on,
enchanted by empty space and holding on to the vision, fighting for blankness. 'You are ours,' the forces of consequence
growled through the night. 'I'm free of all of it. Free from
everything,' Jacob countered. But the webs of consequence
remained tightly wound around his heart and the night slowly
wore on until at last morning threatened.

By dawn Jacob knew that he would not be heading north.
Exhausted by the struggle, he acknowledged the way of the
world, its power, its inescapability, even, perhaps, its desirability, but he had seen something else, a pit or a summit, and that
would never go away entirely, the excitement and the terror of
being nothing more than an iota, a particle, a creature without
meaning in a great accidental void. That remained to him like a
secret self, another being. He was not the same. Not Jacob
coming to his senses and returning to his old self, but changed.
Not renewed, but remade as someone who walked for ever on a
line between the temptations of despair and the pragmatics of

life. When he crossed back over the Jabbok to confront his brother, he would take with him a dark debilitating secret twin who had been born out of his struggle.

Perhaps, after all, the Lord had come to him that night, marshalling his created forces of human emotional ties and all that derives from them, the impetus, the impotence, everything that keeps humanity's heart beating doggedly in the face of the absurd. Perhaps this was how the voice of the Lord – after it had been challenged and silenced by Abraham's great bluff, if that was what it was – now was heard: obliquely, through the tangle of human obligation. All the sticky compelling power of love, hate and betrayal, summoning up a voice that offers nothing but a continuation of all that as an alternative to the blank pointlessness of nature pure and simple. A cunning Lord, maybe, or a cunning editor who makes him so. Whatever it may have been, Jacob was blessed that night and weakened, too, as humanity is blessed and weakened by the way of the world. Jacob and the world (or the Lord) came to some sort of accommodation. The price that Jacob had to pay was the debilitating acceptance of meaning. As to the world (or the Lord), who can say?

To Leah's eyes, weakened by a lifetime of weeping and myopic with disappointment, Jacob was unchanged the next morning. True, he did return to his obligations, but then what creature could have contemplated living with himself after abandoning dependants to their fate – to return was an act of no more than elementary humanity. Still, he made a meal of it.

'I have struggled with great forces, with the angel of the Lord,' he announced grandly to his wives and children. 'I am

191

not to be called Jacob any longer, I am renamed Israel – the Lord has changed my name as he changed the name of my grandfather before me. It is a sign and a blessing.'

Then he proved, to Leah at least, that he was the Jacob of old. He divided his family into groups and arranged them for the onward journey south. The concubines, Bilhah and Zilpah and their children were placed at the front of the column, then came Leah and her children and finally, at the back, Rachel and Joseph. If Esau had violence on his mind, it might be assuaged by the time it came to those Jacob – oh yes, it was Jacob, all right – truly loved. It was something, at least, that Leah did not head the column, but the sons of a legally if trickily married wife had to come before (or in this particular case, after) the children of concubines. He was man enough to head the procession himself. But the sound of Rachel and Joseph behind her and her children would have broken Leah's heart if she had had one intact.

The Lord knows that Esau deserved an apology, but Jacob's terror was more visible than his contrition, even though, as soon as Esau and his regiment of men came into view, he fell to his knees and bowed to the ground seven times before his brother came to a halt in front of him. Silence hung heavily in the air while Esau dismounted and stood still, facing Jacob.

And Esau ran towards his brother, lifted him off the ground and wrapped him in his powerful arms, pressing his eyes and forehead against Jacob's shoulder. Jacob remained stiff and still, his arms at his sides, his face impassive, still uncertain. When Esau raised his head from Jacob's unyielding shoulder, his eyes were wet and red with tears. He saw the waiting column behind Jacob, and asked, 'My brother, who are these people with you?'

'My children, my lord, the children that God has been good

enough to bless me with.' And, strictly formal, Jacob motioned his family to come forward in their reverse order and bow in front of their brother-in-law and uncle.

'And all that livestock your servants brought to me?'

'Gifts in the hope you would decide not to harm me and mine.'

Esau stood back and stiffened now, his dark eyes still filled with liquid, but narrowing and seeing more clearly. His voice was colder.

'I've got enough for my needs. Keep what you have. It wasn't why I came to meet you.'

'No, my Lord, I beg you to take this tribute from me, I know it can mean nothing to you, but you have received me kindly and, anyway, I have done well in my life. I have everything.'

Esau turned his palms upward to indicate that he would take the gifts, though they weren't important. His gift of tears had been rejected, but he tried once again to offer fraternity in place of righteous anger.

'You are going back to Canaan? Why don't we travel south together, my brother? Your party and mine.'

'My lord.' Jacob drew a long breath; he managed a kind of smile, stiff and formal. 'My lord, you know what children are like. They don't travel well, and the sheep and cattle are nursing young and exhausted. They can't travel at your pace, and as they are my responsibility, I'd better stay with them. You go home and I'll bring the children and livestock on slowly to your territory at Seir where we can spend some time together.'

'Well, let me leave some of my men with you as an escort.'

'I wouldn't dream of putting you to the trouble, my lord.'

Esau stared long and hard at his brother, as if he were waiting for him to say or do something. Jacob merely held his brittle smile politely and remained silent, still waiting for the attack. There was a question in Esau's eyes, a puzzlement, a problem of recognition. Then when Jacob's frozen smile and cautious look remained unchanged, Esau blinked as if something was in his eye – a piece of grit, or a tear or perhaps he was blinking away the notion that his beginnings and those with whom he had shared them were more important than ancient anger. New beginnings, it seemed, were more important than old ones.

'Well, brother,' was all he said, his voice gruff with disappointment.

'Well, my lord,' answered Jacob, still wary, not realising that his timid rejection of the forgiveness of his twin had made him, in Esau's eyes, not worth the effort of vengeance which, in any case, Esau had lost his taste for.

Esau led his men back towards the land of Seir. When he had gone, Jacob rearranged his caravan and headed towards Succoth, which was not in the direction of Seir. Nor, Leah noted with interest, was it the way towards Hebron and the father Jacob had not seen for so many years.

He had survived. After all this time, and all the dread, he had come away from the meeting with his brother with his life and goods intact. The relief was like a boulder lifted from his neck – but only for a moment. This long terror having been endured and overcome gave him no more than a brief reprieve, not the absolute release he had expected. Indeed, after the initial sense of freedom there was a feeling of anticlimax, of merely having taken a single hurdle in his race. Now he was free to dread the next. Would there never be any rest, any way he could settle his life into a completed achievement and enjoy the peace he surely deserved? And what was it he dreaded? He told himself he didn't know. The dread seeped back into his consciousness, bearing down on him at least as weightily as the anxiety he'd felt of meeting the brother he once cheated. So it was not that. Something else. A doom, even after he had come through what he most feared, that sat in his head and heart and would not let him enjoy the peace of mind which he had come now to see as his single goal. Still, viscerally, in a place inside himself that he thought of as a locked room, he waited for the catastrophe which for a second he allowed himself to imagine had passed. The thing he could not face, the burden of sadness he would not be able to bear. And still he could not understand what it was.

It was without a second thought that he headed the caravan toward Succoth – not solely to avoid another meeting with Esau, but to build sheds for his cattle and shelter for his people which suggested he intended to remain there for a season at least. He did not think about the fact that he had been going, originally, to Hebron, to the land of his fathers. He *was* going to Hebron. He would go to Hebron. But nonetheless he settled his family and his livestock in Succoth, which was not on the road to home.

There were no complaints at first – none of the party had ever been to Hebron and had no ties with it, there was no great anxiety to arrive at their destination. But eventually, after a year had passed and another threatened to, Rachel demanded a plan.

'What are we doing here? Is this where we are staying? What if your father dies? How can we take our rightful place in Hebron if we are settled somewhere else?'

Even if it was a strange land for Rachel, Hebron was Jacob's birthright and therefore Joseph's – youngest in time though he might be. Rachel wanted to be the mistress of the homeland

and to ease her son into his inheritance as her aunt had done before her.

Jacob seemed surprised. Was there somewhere else to go? Were they still on a journey? Wasn't it perfectly pleasant where they were? Rachel wondered if he had become simple with age.

'Have you forgotten, you were going home? Back to your father—'

'Well, we'll move on then,' said Jacob, cutting her off, but without enthusiasm.

They got as far as Salem, which was at least in Canaan. Here Jacob bought some land just outside the town, from the local ruler, Hamor, where he pitched his tents and began to look every bit as settled as he had in Succoth. He had simply delayed returning home – elsewhere. Rachel wondered if, far from growing simple, he had some cunning plan perhaps to accumulate land. It had to be one or the other. Simple or cunning, with Jacob it was hard to tell.

Leah had no great desire to get to where they were supposed to be going. Salem was as good or bad a place as any. Nothing would change for her wherever they were. She had her family, her boys and her daughter, and that was all she had. Well, it was more than many women had. It was only her foolish childhood dreams that had given her the notion that a good life required love. Yes, she had the love of her children, but they were not *other*, they were not from another place, separate souls who looked and saw and wept at the sight of her, recognising her. She was unloved by the man who had loved her sister with all the passion and devotion she had hoped for herself. It was wrong; scandalously wrong, outrageously wrong, and no amount of time passing would reconcile Leah to the terrible

196

error. She said she had more than many women, but minute by minute she suffered rage at the unjustness of her existence. It was not that she lost her chance of Jacob's love by tricking him into marriage; he would never have loved her. She did not even have herself to blame. He had never recognised who she really was. A dreadful mistake had been made. Nothing would ever rectify it. What did Leah care whether they were in Salem or Hebron?

She hardly wondered if her daughter dreamed of a grand future, as she once did. Dinah was now approaching the age when Leah had first set eyes on Jacob and recognised the love she had been waiting for. They were not close, Leah and Dinah. Leah watched the growing child warily, as if she dared not know her thoughts; there was room in her leaden heart only for her own suffering, she could not encompass a girl child's hopes which might, like hers, be shattered. It was as near as Leah could get to loving Dinah. The girl was too like herself. She was not particularly pretty or good at gaining the attention of the world, and there was an inwardness, a daydreaming, absent-minded look. As a child, she played alone a good deal of the time. She was the only daughter of Jacob, but there were other girls among the servants and workers that she might have been friendly with. For the most part, she kept to herself. She had Rachel's, not her mother's eyes. There was nothing weak about Dinah's eyes. Their dreaminess was not a pale wateriness, but violet pools that darkened around the edges of the pupils to the deepest of midnight blue. Astonishing eyes in a nondescript face that made those who were inclined not to notice her at first glance stop suddenly and turn round once she had passed them by. Rachel's eyes, Leah's inwardness.

*

Dinah was not an unhappy child, not a child who suffered agonies from comparison with a sister, but she was a lonely soul. Her older brothers were fond enough of her, teasing her affectionately when they were around, but they were working youths learning their trades, and she was, after all, only a girl. Jacob had found himself interested in her. Something about the way she wandered alone around the compound, seeming contented and contained, as if deep in thought, intrigued him. He knew nothing of girl children. He wondered about her in spite of himself, touched even by the solemn, solitary pacings of one so small. Perhaps she reminded Jacob of himself when he was a boy and preparing, as he thought, for a life of study in tents. He was shocked by the memory. By now he had forgotten that there had been any life, especially the life of a young thoughtful mind, before he served up the lentil stew to his idiotic brother.

'Hello,' he said, speaking to her deliberately for the first time.

Dinah lifted her face up to him and he caught the blaze of her eyes in their unremarkable surround. He almost gasped. He saw whose eyes they were immediately. She continued to look up at him, mildly curious but saying nothing.

'What are you doing?'

'Playing.'

'But you are just walking.'

'Playing in my head.'

'Don't you play with toys? Doesn't your mother give you dolls?'

'It's better in my head. Realer.'

'Really?'

She nodded emphatically. Jacob remembered suddenly how real playing in his head had been.

'What are you playing?'

She shook her head at him. It was private.

'Do you know who I am?'

She looked at him as if he were foolish.

'You're my father. You live with Aunt Rachel and Joseph.' To Jacob's ears the second statement implied a negation of the first.

'Still, I'm your father. And you are my only daughter. The only girl. And you have beautiful eyes.'

Dinah made a face, pushing her bottom lip forward and raising her eyebrows high. Jacob laughed.

'You don't seem impressed. Perhaps we had better get to know each other better?'

'You mean I would come to your quarters to see you?'

Jacob thought of Rachel's reaction to a child of Leah's, even the girl child, making visits to their quarters. He thought also that such familiarity with the daughter might make the child's mother believe that he had drawn closer to her.

'We could talk when we meet up, like we have today.'

The child shrugged her neutrality at the *could* and *when* of accident.

'I must be getting along,' Jacob said awkwardly, discomforted by the half-heartedness of both of them. 'There are things I must supervise.'

Dinah watched her father disappearing towards the fields for a second and then returned to her interior games.

Several years passed, during which far from meeting up with Dinah and getting to know her, Jacob had actually avoided the child when he saw her. She interested him, but disturbed him, too, and of all things he didn't want to be disturbed. By the time they arrived at Salem with the fear of Esau no longer nagging at Jacob, and the extraordinary news that Rachel was expecting another child, Dinah was a girl on the verge of womanhood whose relationship with her father was no closer than it had been during that first conversation between them.

She still liked to walk, daydreaming and proposing narratives in her head. She no longer called it playing. She had no word for it now. But it was still private. Even so, she wondered about the girls of her own age in the town of Salem, if there might not be some or one, like her, who walked and told themselves stories, who might want to walk with her, and perhaps talk about the things that neither of them talked about to anyone else. She imagined having a friend and grew so beguiled with the idea of someone, like herself, waiting to be found, that she took to entering the town and wandering about, watching for other girls. There were plenty to be seen, but they had made their friendships. Girls walked arm in arm, huddled together, whispering and giggling, and at best gave her cool sidelong glances that made it clear there was no room for outsiders in their groupings. In any case, what was a girl from the outskirts doing here, walking in the town on her own?

But as well as looking she was also seen. The lord of the area, Hamor, from whom Jacob had bought his land outside the town, had a son called Shechem, who was only a little older than Dinah. He saw Dinah in the streets and wondered, like the girls, who she was and why she was alone. Girls never walked about alone in Salem. He began to look out for her although she was not pretty, nothing like as exciting as the town girls who lowered their eyes when they caught up with him in a parody of modesty as enticing as if they walked naked before him, and then swung their hips gently from side to side when they had gone beyond him. But the games the local girls played were old; this strange girl, unthinkably alone, was new and in her solitariness and her obliviousness to his presence nearby on the street more interesting than what was teasingly offered to him by the more self-conscious girls. There was no great hurry for him to marry, he was still very young, but quite soon he would take a wife, and the girls of the town, even knowing that Shechem's wife would be a careful dynastic choice by Hamor, hoped it might be them. Just as the Salem girls found ways to cross Shechem's path several times a day, so Shechem presented himself to the one from outside the town. He received not so much as a glimmer of recognition from her, and used as he was to being noticed by girls he was both intrigued and annoyed. Who was she, he asked himself back at home in his princely house, to look through him as if he didn't exist? She was nothing special to look at, that was certain (though he had noticed by now the deep violet eyes), and no one his father would countenance having as a daughter-in-law – though why he should have such a thought about a total stranger, he could not imagine. He realised after following her that she was the daughter of the leader of the party from Paddan-aram, nomads who had decided to buy some of his father's land and settle. They had a little wealth, but none of the power and respect locally which Shechem's family had consolidated over the decades. Upstarts, nobodies who thought a packet of land was enough. But the plain daughter of the nomad who walked his town played on Shechem's mind. He was angry at his invisibility to her and the look she had on her face suggesting she had much more interesting things on her mind than him. His anger concentrated into a furious desire to invade the private world that prevented her from noticing him. A rush of violence in him wanted to tear her privacy away, to sully the place in her that lived contentedly without needing to know him.

Finally, he did not allow her to pass him by. He stood four-square in her way on the street and, absorbed in her own internal world as she was, she almost walked straight into him. Dinah gasped at finding herself back in reality and at the near collision, as well as at the lack of decorum of her situation. She lowered her eyes. Shechem stood in front of her, barring her way, saying nothing. She looked at him at last. He returned her stare.

'What are you doing?' he demanded.

'Walking.'

'Alone?'

'I like to walk alone.'

'Then why not walk alone where no one can see you? Girls of your age aren't supposed to be unaccompanied in the street.'

'And boys of your age aren't supposed to talk to girls they don't know.'

'So why don't you walk somewhere else, away from the sight of other people?'

It was a good question. Because she wanted a friend, but she had not thought it might be a boy, nor one who seemed so angry.

'So it's up to me to prevent you from doing what you're not supposed to do?' she said, fighting back.

'You draw attention to yourself. It's not the way around here.'

Shechem was enjoying the banter with the girl, but still the secret place behind her eyes evaded him.

'My father is Hamor.'

Dinah had nothing to say.

'Come home with me. We can talk.'

It was unthinkable. Yet Dinah had wandered unthinkably alone through the streets of Salem in the hope that she might find a friend. What if this boy were her friend? He had come to her, interrupted her solitude with an invitation to talk. And who, apart from Jacob, just that once, had ever done that? His anger now looked more like intensity. The directness of his outrageous demand suggested to Dinah that they might indeed have something to share with one another.

'I'm Shechem, son of Hamor.'

'Dinah, daughter of Leah.'

Leah's sons claimed that their sister was raped, but Leah herself was not so sure. Certainly, the youth had taken Dinah to his bed, a virgin, unmarried, a mere girl. It was a family disgrace, a social outrage. The boys spoke of it in hushed tones when their mother was present, suppressing their dynastic anger in order to protect her feelings. But outrage was at the core of Leah's life. Each of her children born in outrage: her struggle for and failure to achieve the regard of their father. Leah did not need protecting from this new version of her old reality. And now Rachel was again big with child and throwing her sister glances of triumph as if this new brat would be her twelfth not her second son. So the family's name was sullied. What did Leah care? Shame was habit to Leah. The boys, when they thought their mother was not in earshot, exploded at the insult in a way they could not explode at the continuing insult to their mother by their father. Even though unloved, especially because unloved, they clung to their birthright, their honour, the family; but Leah remained a stranger. Now her daughter had experienced a travesty of love. Perhaps it is what happens to solitary girls who live their young lives inside their heads. But Dinah's thoughts about what had happened were unknown. She was still at the house of Hamor and Shechem.

Hamor arrived, grim and solemn, accompanied only by his

son, to speak to Jacob. Dinah's brothers ran back from the fields to hear what they had to say about their absent sister. Like Jacob's mother before her, Leah listened outside the meeting room to what was being said about her child.

'He loves her,' explained Hamor, an older man talking to an older man of youth. 'He says she is his soul, his being. He will have no other wife. So let Dinah be his wife. It would make your family and mine allies – we'll intermarry and you will be properly settled here, travel about freely and own more land. It makes sense to us as fathers and heads of our households. To the boy, there is no sense, he is senseless with love.'

Jacob was silent. Then Shechem spoke.

'Please, sir, I beg you, let me marry her. I'll give anything to be her husband, whatever you ask as a bride price, any amount as a gift to her family. Just let us be married.'

Jacob was silent still. Leah knew that Shechem, having violated her, was obliged to marry Dinah, and that he had to pay whatever the offended family demanded, but she was struck by his tone of voice. He was not only saying what had to be said, but begging like a besotted lover for Dinah's hand. He did love her, Leah was as sure of that as she had been sure of Jacob's love for Rachel when he talked to her about it all those years ago. Leah heard the young voice of Shechem and felt suddenly dizzy with remembering her interior voice which had spoken love to her as a child which she had confused with her love for Jacob. It was the voice of love she had heard, not the voice of Jacob. Now she heard it again from the boy Shechem's lips about her daughter. She felt a pang of regret that it was not for her. How could she feel the social disgrace her sons felt when such a declaration was what she had longed for all her life? Was her daughter violated or loved? Who could say if the boy had forced her to have sex with him, or if Dinah had been willing to investigate friendship as fully as possible? Only Dinah, and no one thought to ask her because the violation remained paramount as far as the family was concerned. Was Dinah held captive by Shechem, who spoke so remarkably of love and soul and offered to do and pay anything to keep her with him, or did she remain with him because she feared the response of her brothers no matter what her wishes and desires? Or had she stayed of her own free will because she loved and was loved? No one asked. What Dinah wanted was not the point. The one boy loved, the other boys were shamed. But the chances were, Leah thought, that Dinah had responded to the voice of love and perhaps even found a voice of her own. The one boy loved, the other boys were shamed, the mother longed. And Dinah? Who could say?

After Shechem's plea, the brothers waited for the wrath of their father, but when it failed to come, when he had stood for a long moment saying nothing to the rapist or his father, the boys were aghast. Was he afraid of the local prince? So fearful of disruption that he would take any insult in silence? Did he so long for peace and quiet that he was considering the possibility of the house of Abraham intermarrying with these Canaanite neighbours and disappearing for ever? Finally, Simeon, the second son, spoke.

'It's out of the question. We can't allow our sister to be married into an uncircumcised family. Only if you agree to have every male in the town circumcised – a gesture of good faith on your part, of faith on ours – can we allow Dinah to marry the Prince Shechem. Then we can settle and marry with you and become one people. But if you won't agree, we will take our sister and go.'

There was a gasp from some of the brothers, but a fierce look from Simeon reminded them that he was no conciliator, and they remained silent until they could talk together. Jacob said nothing.

Shechem and his father immediately agreed and set off back to the town to talk to the men, leaving Jacob alone with his sons. Leah stood now in the entrance, no longer bothering to conceal herself. The brothers stared at Jacob, who seemed physically to shrink under their gaze. He had lost his place among them, Leah could see. In just those few moments Jacob had become an old man, fearful, dithering, no longer the head of the household, and the boys had become men. They towered over Jacob, a small man grown smaller, and Leah's sons took up the role of leaders of the family. Jacob, who would not love where love belonged, weakened into ineffectual old age. It gave Leah no pleasure, but a grim triumph bloomed in her.

This moment was the birth of the enfeebled old man who now wept inconsolably over the loss of his beloved son Joseph. It was the reunion with his father he had been dreading so much that he had been unable to lead his household home. Yet here was Isaac, fearful, filled with doubt, encountered in his own being. There was no need to go back to Hebron to meet Isaac, he had his father with him all along, blood and bone close, just as he had feared while still a boy living in tents. In front of his contemptuous sons, Jacob felt his eyes dim and his body weaken under the weight of terror – he braced himself for pain and loss, made himself small in the face of the might of tragedy. His mind had gone quite blank when he stood between Hamor asking for alliance yet threatening his security, and his sons, fiery young grandsons of the house of Abraham, not of the sickbed of Isaac, threatening his peace. Silence and absence of thought was all he could come up with confronted with the fact of his daughter's disgrace and the demand on him to do something about it. He did not think of Dinah or the family name, but only that the Lord of Abraham had betrayed him, had given him this difficulty instead of being with him and ensuring his well-being. *Why* was he being treated like this? Why wasn't his way being smoothed? He was old, he had had a hard life, done the best he could; surely he deserved some consideration. And anyway, there had been promises: to his grandfather, to his father, to him.

And during his silence the sons decided that Shechem was not to be punished, and that the two households were to merge. *The sons decided. The sons of Leah.* Well, so be it. This was to be the end of Abraham's dynasty – a merging with another people. Jacob could hardly care. What had Abraham ever done for him apart from give him Isaac for a father? Why should Jacob care if Abraham's seed and his Lord's promises disappeared into the sand of the desert? And it would be best this way for Jacob. There would be no unpleasantness, no requirement for revenge. No need to move on and be forced to return to Hebron. The boy, Shechem, seemed a well-intentioned lad. Dinah could do worse. The family could do worse. And Shechem was just a youth. He had had a moment of madness, perhaps, his passion difficult to control at such an age. Yet he had respect for the girl. He had to marry her, of course, but he seemed to want to. Should he have to wait seven years to achieve his heart's desire? What good had it done Jacob, that long wait for love? Let the boy show his sincerity and goodwill by circumcising himself and his followers and be done with it. Let the scandal be smoothed over. It was best this way. He could go back to a peaceful life with Rachel and his son, Joseph and the new child to come.

But peace and uneventfulness were never going to settle on Jacob. There was to be only turmoil from now until the end. Simeon was no peace-maker, and two days after Hamor, Shechem and the men of Salem had voluntarily circumcised themselves and were still in great pain and weakened, he and Levi, the third son of Jacob, strode into town in the early hours, and in a frenzy of revenge all the more pitiless for it having to be suppressed until this moment, they broke down the doors of the houses and slaughtered every man they found. Hamor and Shechem, also nursing their circumcision wounds, rose from their beds in the palace at the commotion, the wailing of the women, the shouts and cries of the men. Simeon and Levi found them at the gates of the palace paralysed with horror and incomprehension at the butchery they saw all around them, and with their sister's name on their lips the two brothers repeatedly rammed their bloodstained swords into the boy and his father. Dinah was discovered huddled with fear under the quilt in Shechem's bed. Simeon and Levi dressed her and took her out of the palace, past the poor mutilated bodies of Hamor and Shechem, through the town of dead and dying men and keening women, where her other brothers were looting and torching the houses with all the zest of the truly righteous. Dinah was brought home to her family. She had made a stran-gled sound in the back of her throat when she saw the body of Shechem, but after that she was silent. Dinah did not speak again.

Jacob, however, found his voice at last.

'What have you done?' he howled at his sons. 'You've made such trouble for me, my name will stink to all the Canaanites.

We're just a handful, compared to them. And Rachel pregnant. If they get together and attack me, I'll be destroyed. The whole household will be destroyed. '

The boys looked at their whining, fearful father, who for so long had looked at them from the distance of his other family. Simeon spoke for them all in a new voice of disdain that Jacob recognised as once his own to *his* father, long ago.

'So as long as nothing disturbs you, it's all right for our sister to be treated like a whore?'

Our sister, not *your daughter*. Well, true enough. And yes, if only life would leave him alone.

Leah laughed out loud when Jacob announced to the gathered household he called together the following morning that God had spoken to him and reminded him that he had not kept the promise he had made at Bethel when he fled from his brother all those years ago, to return there and build an altar to the Lord.

'Another dream voice?' Leah called out.

'Spoke to me,' Jacob insisted sullenly. 'And my wives and their servants have displeased the Lord with their worship of alien gods. It has to change. Destroy your icons. We will go to Bethel and you will worship only the God of Abraham. Is that clear?'

Leah, who would worship any god or none for all the good any of them did her, laughed again.

'And this has nothing to do with the hordes you think are gathering to attack us for revenging Dinah?'

'The Lord has spoken. Get things packed up. We leave immediately.'

The voice of authority. Or the voice of fear mimicking authority.

So they left Salem with an urgency, to keep Jacob's promise of more than two decades ago, or to save their lives. After the events in Salem, everyone felt safer on the road. Once they arrived, Jacob went off alone and kept himself unavailable building the altar to the Lord in Bethel, in the place where he had once curled up small in the terrifying desert dark. When it was done he returned to society to announce that God had come again, to remind everyone that his name was now Israel, not Jacob, and that he had been assured that the land they were in would be his. The members of the family nodded, but no one ever thought to call him anything but Jacob.

They did not stay in Bethel. Their wanderings, it seemed, had begun again. Jacob's hope of a quiet, sedentary life had been shattered in Salem, and it looked as if he dare not rest for fear of some other terrible event disrupting his life. He seemed to think that uneventfulness was better to be found in move-ment. Jacob said that they were making their way back to Hebron and 'home' as he called it, but Leah doubted that they were making their way to any final destination.

They were on the road that led to Ephrath when Rachel went into labour. Leah did not attend her sister, there were nurses and midwives enough. She kept watch on the birthing tent from a distance and saw Jacob sitting outside it. It was a long vigil. Leah had never laboured so long or cried out in such pain. Rachel had been determined to have children, just the one boy would not do. 'Give me sons,' she had cried out to Jacob. Even though she had the love, Leah thought bitterly, still it pained her that Leah had the children who would ensure the future of Abraham, Isaac and Jacob's line. Leah would be the mother of future generations. Even when she had Joseph she was not sat-isfied. One child only served to terrify Rachel. Joseph was nurtured and coddled, the precious singleton, but all the care in the world could not guarantee that he would survive. Once there was one child, there had to be another, at least another. For certainty. Leah remembered feeling the same way. If each child would not make Jacob love her, it would at least ensure her place. What catastrophe could take six sons away from her? Leah understood what Rachel wanted. The fear of the mother with a single child was like a woman who walked the edge of a cliff in terror of any wind that might blow her off into the chasm below. The chasm of childlessness. A death more absolute than death itself. Wasn't that the reason for the house of Abraham and its generations? The only future lay in the next generation and memory. So Rachel had to have another even though Rachel had everything. At least everything that Leah had wanted. Why couldn't she be satisfied with love? Because she did not want what Leah wanted. Jacob's love puffed her up, but it didn't satisfy her hunger as nothing else – not even a tribe of sons – would satisfy Leah's hunger. Listening to her sister's birthing screams, Leah now wondered if she would have swapped her life and her children for Rachel's. And she knew she would have given all her sons, and her daughter, let them never exist, let her future die with her body, just so long as she could have Jacob's love. Let Rachel have the babies and grow solid in repute and matriarchal. Leah would not have demanded a single one. How wrong it all was. The thought of the wrongness of her life drained any pity for the cries of her sister as they rang, hour after hour, around the temporary encampment. Leah hated this infant who would consolidate the true family of Jacob, the family of which she and her children could never be part.

*

211

In her anger, Leah did not hear in Rachel's cries the realisation that she had wanted too much. Jacob heard. At least he heard a note in her screams, different from her cries at the birth of Joseph, and it was a knife in his heart. He heard the sound of despair, of one who is already falling into a pit. It was not the pain of childbirth she cried out against. He ran into the tent, but the midwife would not let him stay. He was there long enough to see the look of terror on his wife's face and that it was matched by the grave looks of her attendants. He knew. He saw she knew. Yet the process which was carrying her away had to continue. There was no stopping this disaster, this black ending. He felt anger rise in him at Rachel, for her insistence on having another child. Couldn't they have cared enough for Joseph to ensure that he was safe? She was old, too old for bearing more children from a body that did so reluctantly anyway. One was enough for him. Why did she have to have more? Because of her sister. Because her jealousy of Leah was greater than her love for Jacob. And then the fury became mixed with the memory of his confident assurance to Laban that whoever had stolen his household gods would die for it. He had since seen the icons among Rachel's things and had refused to think about the matter any further. He was not a superstitious man, not really, not even a believer. Only one who took care, just in case. He had not taken enough care that day. Now, the thief was in her death throes. Jacob put his head in his hands and wept for the tragedy that was about to overtake him.

The child was called Benjamin, a motherless creature who lay exhausted in his nurse's arms. Rachel died. Jacob kept the child with him, close, insisting to his nurse that he was always within sight and earshot so that he could know the boy was well and safe. Only Joseph and Benjamin existed now for Jacob. They were the last delicate remnants of love. The household was run by Leah's sons. Jacob reduced his concern with the world to the two children of his lost beloved, Rachel.

Rachel was buried there on the road to Ephrath where she had died and Benjamin had been born. Jacob placed a stone pillar over her grave and made a final authoritative announcement. They would pack up and continue with their journey. The sons of Leah shrugged. Why not, Bethel was nothing to them. They were content to leave behind the grave of the woman who had caused their mother such suffering and made them into secondary sons, blood-tied workmen, to their father. Let the old man have his two favoured molly-coddled children, they had the strength to keep the house of Abraham moving forward. It was time that they took control. Jacob did not care, weakened further and made more frail by his loss and his continuing fear of life's dangers.

He hardly cared when one morning he saw Reuben emerge from Bilhah's tent. There was a cool, almost amused look on Reuben's face when he saw his father looking at him. Rachel was dead, and now his oldest son had taken over his concubine – Rachel's servant, the mother of two of Jacob's children. The handover of power was complete. Leah had survived Rachel and her sons had taken control. What did he need a woman for? Jacob was no more than an ineffectual old man who fussed over two motherless, spoiled children. The baby babbled and Joseph chattered precociously about his dreams and his grand plans once he was old enough to make his usefully strong, but loutish brothers see that they needed a wise and cunning mind directing their labours. Jacob nodded indulgently. It would be so. Joseph was everything a firstborn should be. Blessing and birthright would be his one day.

213

Yet how disappointing life had turned out to be for the infant who boldly clung to his brother's heel to ensure that he would not be left behind in his journey into life. All the dangers, all the risks Jacob had taken, such love, such work, so much manoeuvring for position, and now this feebleness, this waiting room of death. Where was the satisfaction of a great household, many strong sons, wealth, all created out of nothing by the cunning and intelligence of Jacob? What was the prize? None. Sadness, fear and death. The blank end that had been so feared by Abraham. What did Jacob care if his blood continued through future generations? His strength had turned to weakness. Old age had brought him nothing but pain and anxiety. What had it all been for? Dreams. Worthless dreams. All that aiming towards the future that turned out to be bile in the mouth. How could he have known? And if he had known, what would he have done?

News came that Isaac had died. So many years after he had dispensed his deathbed blessing, ever-imminent death had finally arrived. Now, at last, they returned to Hebron. It was necessary, of course, for the son to bury the father, and Jacob's sons were eager, on hearing the news, to return to the land of their birthright, to settle and work the land that Abraham's Lord had promised his heirs. Jacob made no complaint. There was no longer any need for him to avoid Hebron. In any case, what he had been avoiding all this time had already come upon him. Why run any longer from his fear of becoming his father? He let his sons lead him to Hebron.

Rebekah, it seemed, had died long since. Jacob had assumed that. Or he had not thought about it very much. Rebekah's favourite son was too absorbed in thoughts of his father to concern himself about the fate of his mother. The servants knew the details of her death, of course, and where she was buried, but Jacob did not ask. The loving parent had vanished into the exile into which she sent her son. All Jacob could think about was the dead parent who had not loved him.

The old man buried the old man with the help of his brother. Esau, the favourite son of Isaac, came from Edom. The two elderly men took one another in. Esau stood tall, his red hair faded with age, an old warrior, a leader. He did not mention their previous meeting to Jacob, nor the fact that Jacob had failed to make his promised visit to his older twin. He did not, at this meeting, embrace Jacob and weep at their reconciliation. If anything, behind his formality, Jacob thought he saw the same look of mild contempt that his sons wore. But perhaps it was nothing more than disengagement. The two men went about their burying and when it was done separated with a nod of the head and ceremonial good wishes. It was clear to both that they would never see each other again. The time had come at last for Jacob to assume the birthright he had bought with a bowl of lentils. He settled into his father's quarters and gathered Rachel's sons close.

And then, after these things, Reuben came breathlessly to Jacob's room with a bloody rag in his hand.

'Do you recognise this? Isn't it part of that fine tunic you gave Joseph?'

The boy had gone at Jacob's bidding to check on his brothers, to see if they were looking after the sheep properly and to report back. Jacob snatched the remnant of cloth from his oldest son's hand and peered at it, bringing it up close to his dim eyes. Beneath the stiff russet stain of dried blood he made out the fine embroidery of the tunic he had had specially made for his

215

beautiful, clever, beloved son. It was Joseph's tunic. It was a bloody rag. Joseph was dead, there could be no doubt. He felt the desiccated blood powdery under his thumb. The tunic torn to pieces and the seventeen-year-old body inside it? Torn to pieces, Reuben was telling him, with his mute piece of material. The beautiful boy. The savagery which caused only this rag to remain. He understood what Reuben was saying. The boy was dead, torn to shreds, devoured by a raging beast – or beasts. Dead, like Rachel.

And Jacob's life was ashes. He mourned and wept for Joseph and for whatever it was that had killed him. He wept at his own deprivation, at the emptiness and wasteland of his life. He kept the child Benjamin with him day and night. Benjamin was all that was left. If once he let him out of his sight, he knew, the savage beast would get him too. At last, there was only terror. The terror of Abraham, Isaac and Jacob.

And from God, the Dreamed One, the great Redactor, the Editor in Chief, there was only silence. What are a handful of generations to him? Just original material gone its own way, good for nothing more than providing the means to pass the time with a little dreaming and a little interim editing.

Acknowledgements

Before and during the writing of this book and its predecessor, *Only Human*, I read a good deal on the subject of Genesis and the making of the Hebrew Bible. There are many writers to whom I am grateful, not least, of course, the committee who produced the Authorised King James Version and the Jewish Publication Society's translation of the *Tanakh*. In particular, I benefited enormously from thinking around the works of Robert Alter – his literary criticism of the Hebrew Bible, and his translation and commentary of *Genesis* (Norton, 1996); Avivah Gottlieb Zornberg's book of meditations, *The Beginnings of Desire – Reflections on Genesis* (Doubleday, 1996); Shalom Spiegel's *The Last Trial* (Jewish Lights, 1993); Louis Ginzberg's *The Legends of the Jews* (Johns Hopkins University Press, 1998), and the collection of essays edited by Robert Alter and Frank Kermode, *The Literary Guide to the Bible* (Fontana, 1997). None of these valuable works, however, should be held responsible for the final outcome of my imaginings.

Now you can order superb titles directly from Virago